What am I doing? Lena wondered, yet she couldn't seem to stop herself. She felt like the camera was tugging at her finger, pulling it until . . .

She pushed the button. And to her total surprise, the Impulse whirred and a piece of film emerged from the slot in the front.

"Hey, I thought there wasn't anything in there!" Abby said.

"There wasn't!" Lena exclaimed. She pulled the undeveloped picture out of the slot and turned the camera around. "This is so weird. It doesn't have film!"

"Maybe there was one last exposure jammed in the works," her dad suggested, glancing at the girls in the rearview mirror.

"Maybe . . ." Lena mumbled.

POISON APPLE BOOKS

The Dead End by Mimi McCoy

This Totally Bites! by Ruth Ames

Miss Fortune by Brandi Dougherty

Now You See Me . . . by Jane B. Mason &
Sarah Hines Stephens

Midnight Howl by Clare Hutton

NOW YOU SEE ME...

by Jane B. Mason &
Sarah Hines Stephens

SCHOLASTIC INC.

New York   Toronto   London   Auckland
Sydney   Mexico City   New Delhi   Hong Kong

No part of this publication may be reproduced, stored in a retrieval system, or transmitted in any form or by any means, electronic, mechanical, photocopying, recording, or otherwise, without written permission of the publisher. For information regarding permission, write to Scholastic Inc., Attention: Permissions Department, 557 Broadway, New York, NY 10012.

ISBN 978-0-545-21513-8

12 11 10 9 8 7 6 5 4 3 2   10 11 12 13 14 15/0

Printed in the U.S.A.   40
First printing, November 2010

To the jam junkies, the thrift mavens, and the shutterbugs we love (you all know who you are!)

— JBM and SHS

CHAPTER ONE

"No way!" Lena Giff exclaimed. She couldn't believe her eyes. There — right in front of her — was the thing she'd been trying to find for almost six months. She was so surprised, she thought she might be imagining the small gray box sitting on the dusty shelf. "Abby! Abby, get over here!" Lena called. She waved her best friend toward the dark corner of the store.

On the other side of the thrift shop, Abigail Starling's micro-braided curls appeared above the edge of an enormous basket of neckties. She'd been rummaging through, looking for a few that would make good headbands. And from the look of it, she'd struck gold. She had several silk ties draped around her neck, and clutched two more paisley-patterned strips in her hand.

"What's up?" Abby called back. Dropping the ties, she began to pick her way through the cluttered store to see what kind of treasure Lena had unearthed. Abby was an experienced thrifter and could practically smell a good find.

While Abby stepped gingerly past broken candelabras and spindle-leg chairs, Lena reached beyond the stack of dusty *National Geographic* magazines to retrieve the find of all finds. When she felt the smooth plastic under her fingertips, she sucked in her breath.

Just a few days ago she had considered giving up on her quest. It had been feeling fruitless, all the searching through junk shops and flea markets for something so specific. And since she and Abby had a "no eBay" rule about treasure hunting, there had been a lot of legwork involved. But now (could it be?!), the search was over. The very item she'd been looking for was being rescued from a shelf next to a cast-off yellow duffel bag. . . .

"The Impulse!" Abby squealed when she saw the Polaroid camera. "I can't believe it!"

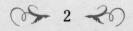

Lena couldn't believe it either, even though she was holding it in her own two hands. It was lighter than expected, and smaller.

"Does it work?" Abby asked excitedly. Her hands were balled into fists and her arms were clamped tightly across her body, as if her excitement might actually leap out of her chest.

All Lena could do was nod. It was the one, all right — the exact model she'd been looking for since March. Cautiously, she pushed the button on the top that turned the camera on and popped up the flash. She peered through the viewfinder, then opened the little door in the front where you inserted the film cartridge.

The good news: The camera wasn't loaded with a corroded film and battery cartridge that had gone gooey and mucked up the works. The bad news: There was no way to know for sure if the camera was functional. Lena would have to trust her luck, buy it, and test the camera out when she got home.

"It looks okay," Lena said in a near whisper, turning the rectangular contraption over. She was so excited, her fingertips were tingling and the hair on her arms was standing up. She'd made some good junk finds before, but this took the cake. And judging by the look on her best friend's face, Abby, the undisputed Queen of Secondhand Scores, thought so, too.

Abby threw up her hands. "Unbelievable. First the lunch box." She waved her tin treasure in the air. "Then the skirt, and now *this*. We are talking serious pay dirt here. I mean, this day could go down in thrift history!"

"Thrifstory?" Lena said with a grin, her green eyes twinkling. Taking a breath, she lifted the camera's strap over her strawberry-blond head. The small box felt surprisingly comfortable hanging around her neck — like it belonged there. The square eye of the viewfinder looked up at her almost expectantly, and Lena felt a sudden urge to get out of the store and get home with her treasure. They hadn't looked through all the store's rooms yet, but the feeling was insistent. Like if she didn't go soon some magic clock might strike midnight, and the camera would turn into a pumpkin and she would be left sitting all alone with one shoe. Or something.

"Let's cash out," Abby suggested before Lena could say anything. It was not like her to propose

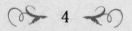

leaving a secondhand shop before every stone (or used suitcase) had been turned. But it *was* just like her to read Lena's mind. The two girls had been best friends since third grade and spent a ton of time together. They even finished each other's sentences. "I just need to gather my haul."

While Lena clutched the camera and fidgeted nervously, Abby darted into another room of the old house-turned-store and emerged with the fashionable finds she had stashed in a corner. Trailing neckties, she ambled across the room and plunked everything down on a large rolltop desk. A gray-haired woman wearing a housecoat looked up from a tattered novel.

"We're ready to check out," Abby said cheerfully.

The woman didn't return her smile, and didn't speak. She simply nodded wearily, picked up a pencil, and switched on the register.

"You first." Abby nudged Lena forward. "You've been waiting a long time for this."

Lena stumbled up to the desk and reached up to remove the camera strap from around her neck. The camera felt heavier now, and though she placed the Impulse on the desk, she didn't let go right away. When she did, she realized that her palms were sweating. She felt as if she were getting a tooth filled or waiting for a shot in the doctor's office.

Probably just excitement, she told herself. Was this what it felt like to win the lottery? *Maybe it's adrenaline. Or shock.* Finding the camera certainly seemed too good to be true. . . .

"Where'd you get this?" the woman at the register spoke for the first time, and Lena flinched, wishing she hadn't. Her voice was loud and harsh. She squinted at Lena and gave the camera a poke with her pen like it was some sort of poisonous insect.

Lena felt her excitement begin to slip away. "I . . . I . . ." she stammered, feeling foolish. She took a step back, bumping into Abby.

Abby's arm collided with the pile of loot on the desk, and half of it slid to the floor.

The woman ignored the fallen items. "Where did you get it?" she screeched. Her steely eyes were narrowed behind her reading glasses and aimed, laserlike, right at Lena.

Lena pointed toward the shelf in the back room where the Impulse had been waiting. "Right over there," she replied. She looked nervously from the back room to the camera, and then to the front door.

She felt sick. She desperately wanted the camera. What if she didn't get it?

Take it and run, a voice in her head told her. *There's no way she could keep up.* But Lena was not a thief! She might drive a hard bargain (not as hard as Abby), but she didn't steal.

While Abby picked her treasures up off the floor, Lena tried to calm herself down. Everything was going to be fine. She'd seen shopkeepers act weird before — they did all kinds of things to convince you your items were worth more than you wanted to pay. *That's all that's happening here,* she thought. She braced herself for a ridiculously high price and wiped her clammy palms on her shorts.

The woman's sharp gaze rested on the camera for several long moments. Then, out of the blue, her face softened. She looked almost . . . sad. But in a flash, her expression changed again. A gnarled hand reached out with alarming speed. "Well, it's not for sale!" she growled, snatching the camera and shoving it under the desk.

Lena felt as though she'd gotten the wind knocked out of her. Finding the Impulse really *was* too good to be true! She wanted to protest, but couldn't. Her bubble had burst. She couldn't speak.

Or move. Or do anything. She might have just stood there deflating for the rest of the day if Abby hadn't piped up behind her.

As usual, Lena's best friend had her back . . . and (in this case) a boatload of potential purchases. "It was *on* the shelf," the bolder girl pointed out.

"Well, that was a mistake," the woman snapped. She obviously didn't appreciate being questioned.

Abby didn't flinch. "Well, I guess these are mistakes, too," she replied calmly. With a flourish, she whisked the 50s dress, huge square-dance crinoline, suspenders, Boy Scout uniform, 'NSYNC lunch box, five ties, and the stack of CDs she had amassed off the rolltop and set them on a rickety table nearby. Half a second later she was arranging the dress on a hanger, prepping it to go back on the rack.

Lena almost smiled. The girl was unflappable. Abby had no intention of leaving her finds behind, Lena knew. And if her stomach wasn't still in a knot, she might have enjoyed the showdown. After all, it appeared to be a pretty even match. The old woman looked fierce, but Abby was a contender.

The woman's steely eyes followed Abby as she started to walk the merchandise back to where she'd found it. Then, with a heavy sigh, she looked around

the crowded, dusty shop. Shaking her head with res-
ignation, she reached back into the desk for the
camera.

"You really want this old thing?" she asked. She
caught Lena's eye and held her gaze. Her voice was
gentler now, and Lena noticed laugh lines around
her eyes. Maybe the old bat wasn't always this
cranky. Maybe she was just having a bad day.

"Yes, I really do," Lena replied with an
emphatic nod.

"Well, all right," the old woman breathed. "I'll let
you have it for five dollars. Maybe it'll be good to be
rid of it."

The woman smoothed a few wild gray hairs
toward the knot at the back of her head while Lena
dug into her pocket and swallowed a victory cry.

Five dollars! I guess I'm stealing after all! She
handed over a five-dollar bill and bit back a smile.
She would have gladly emptied her whole wallet
for the camera if she had to. But she knew it was
never good to let the seller see how much you want
something. She should simply consider the five-
dollar price tag a bonus and keep her excitement to
herself.

The moment the bill left Lena's fingers, she

grabbed the camera and slipped the strap back around her neck. She let the Impulse rest against her side. The weight, though nothing like her digital camera, was at once familiar and comforting. She breathed a sigh of relief. It was hers. The Impulse was finally hers!

CHAPTER TWO

Exhilarated, the girls emerged from the dim shop into the early autumn sun. Lena's dad was leaning against the hood of the family station wagon, waiting patiently. When he saw the big bags of stuff they were carrying, he shook his head and scuffed through the thin layer of fallen leaves to open the car door.

"Your parents are never going to let me take you with me again," he told Abby, laughing as he bent over to make room in the backseat.

"Breathe easy, Mr. G.," Abby replied, giving him a reassuring pat on the back. "My parents are familiar with my thrifting, er, problem — they won't blame you."

Lena hoped not. It would be a total bummer if

Abby couldn't come treasure hunting every end of summer. Their weekend farm-town visits during peach, berry, and apple season were September highlights. And Phelps, the town they were in now, was Lena's personal favorite. The funky farm village just outside the larger city of Narrowsburg, where they all lived, was known for its antiques and luscious fruit.

Lena felt a chill as she climbed into the car, which surprised her. She'd been sweltering all day. But now, standing in the shade, she was practically shivering. She wished she'd brought a sweater.

Abby folded herself into the car behind Lena, her face aglow. Lena tried to ignore the shivers so she could bask in the celebratory mood that emanated from her friend. Even though Abby hadn't been able to talk the store owner into throwing in the ties for free, Lena could tell that she was feeling victorious. Considering that half the backseat was covered in new treasures and she was only out eighteen bucks, she should.

Abby was a professional thrifter. Both girls had been honing their skills for three years, and now, at age twelve, they were experts at finding bargains and negotiating deals. But Abby took it to the next level. She could sniff out a good find like a hound dog, and was a fierce negotiator when it came to price.

How funny that it all started by accident, Lena mused as she sat back and tried to absorb the warmth of the sunshine streaming through the window. They'd been having one of many playdates at Lena's house when Mr. Giff announced that the strawberries were ripe and he had to go to Phelps for a couple of flats. (Mr. Giff was a jam-making nut who would drive through four states for a good berry or the last peaches of the season.) Back then the girls were too young to stay home alone, so they had no choice but to go along. They'd complained loudly, but the trip turned out to be a total blast. They loaded up on berries, then hit Mr. Giff's favorite thrift store, where they found a whole collection of old Barbie dolls for practically nothing. That was all it took to get them hooked on bargain hunting.

Now the trio picked the country towns clean at the end of each summer. And this year — including today's trip — was no exception.

"I've got all my flats tucked in safe and sound," Mr. Giff announced from the front seat. "You girls get everything loaded up?"

"Sure did, Mr. G.," Abby replied as she closed the door. "We're ready to roll."

As the car pulled out of the little parking lot, Lena stared out the window, her hands folded on top of the camera. She was still thrilled to have it, but could not deny the cold whisper of worry that had descended upon her. The old lady's reaction to selling the camera had definitely been severe. Lena wondered again what had prompted her to get so . . . angry. And what had made her sell the camera after all? Did she need the money? Business must be slow in sleepy Phelps. But then why would she sell the camera for so little?

Never mind, Lena told herself. *The important thing is that the camera is mine!* She forcefully steered her thoughts out of the shadows toward happier things — like all the fabulous stuff she was going to photograph with her new camera — and watched the familiar trees and fields flash past outside her window.

Beside her, Abby inspected her loot. "Check this out," she said, pointing to the tag on the square-dancing skirt. "Josie-Do's, get it? Like do-si-do?" The skirt had so many layers, Abby was practically hidden behind it. She had to smash it down to look at the rest of her bargains.

"So, what do you think I should put in my lunch box?" she asked, running her slender fingers over Justin Timberlake's face. "My nail polish collection?"

"You could use it for, you know . . . lunch," Lena suggested.

"Brilliant!" Abby sang. "See? That is precisely why you are my best friend — nonstop great ideas."

Lena smiled distractedly and turned back toward the window just in time to see a large U-Pick strawberry patch that was closed for the season. Long, mounded rows ran from the side of the road toward the horizon, surrounded on three sides by huge wild rose hedges. It looked just like a dozen other berry fields Lena had seen in the area — nothing special.

But before she even knew what was happening, Lena had raised her new camera to her eye.

What am I doing? Lena wondered. Aside from the long shadows cast by the hedges, the field was fairly flat and featureless. Kind of lonely looking, really, filled with withered berry plants and a boarded-up stand. There was no stark contrast to capture, no strong figure, no story in the frame. And yet she couldn't seem to stop herself. She felt like the camera was tugging at her finger, pulling it until . . .

She pushed the button. And to her total surprise, the Impulse whirred and a piece of film emerged from the slot in the front.

"Hey, I thought there wasn't anything in there!" Abby said, looking up and leaning over to peer at the vintage contraption.

"There wasn't!" Lena exclaimed. She pulled the undeveloped picture out of the slot and turned the camera around. Sliding the button to release the little door, she looked inside. Sure enough, the battery/film compartment was still empty — no used cartridge, nothing. "This is so weird. It doesn't have film!" She shook her head, baffled, and handed the camera to Abby for additional inspection, leaning sideways so she wouldn't have to take off the strap.

"Maybe there was one last exposure jammed in the works," her dad suggested, glancing at the girls in the rearview mirror.

"Maybe . . ." Lena mumbled. She squinted at the shot. "But I doubt it'll turn out. I mean, the film has to be expired. And it wasn't even in a cartridge." Not to mention the fact that she took the picture out the window of a moving car. Blur city.

Still, Lena studied the grayish square to see if anything would show up.

Abby bent closer so she could watch, too. Neither of them breathed as out of the black, shades of blue, and then green began to emerge. Lena watched as forest-colored leaves appeared, then roses, and . . . something else.

Lena blinked, trying to figure out what it was. "Did you guys notice a water tower in that field?" she asked.

"Sorry, sweetie, I wasn't really paying attention," her dad apologized.

"Missed it," Abby shrugged.

Lena stared at the water tower growing clearer in the photo. It was one of the old-fashioned kinds, all metal, with four long, sturdy legs that looked like triangular ladders and a round tank for the water on top. The name of the town, PHELPS, was painted in giant red letters across the front of the tank. In the picture it stood in the center of the field. But in real life . . .

"I swear that wasn't there when we went by," Lena said, baffled. "It was just rows of plants, the hedge, and a boarded-up shack where the berries were sold." She could hear her voice rising along with the goose bumps popping up on her arms. Now she was *really* chilled.

Abby looked at Lena with concern. "I believe you; I just wasn't looking," she said.

Lena's dad was busy tuning into something on the car radio and tuning out what was going on in the backseat.

"Dad, go back," Lena pleaded, leaning toward the front seat. "Please? I have to see if that tower was there."

"Wish I could, but we're already late," her dad replied. "I told your mom we'd be back by five thirty for dinner. Maybe you just didn't see it." He shrugged. "Or maybe it's some sort of double exposure."

Lena flopped back against the backseat and looked again at the tower standing in the center of her instant picture. It hadn't been there. She was sure of it.

CHAPTER THREE

"Okay, okay, now give me glam." Lena directed Abby the way she imagined a real fashion photographer might. "I want attitude," she said. She was trying to sound serious, but the harder she tried to keep a straight face, the more she smirked. Before long the two of them were cracking up.

Their Polaroid photo session, being conducted on the sidewalks of Narrowsburg, was hardly a glamorous fashion shoot in Milan. Getting the giggles was definitely allowed. And in spite of the silliness, Lena thought Abby looked pretty cool posing in front of the retro-looking brick building on Second Street. The late morning light was perfect, the sky was full of puffy white clouds, and the cool breeze that came and went ruffled Abby's skirt like a wind machine, fluffing it perfectly.

Abby's vintage ensemble, courtesy of yesterday's thrift and freshened by last night's wash, was even managing to resemble cutting-edge fashion.

If a Boy Scout uniform and a pound of puffy skirts can be considered cutting edge, Lena thought, stifling another laugh.

"Looks fab," she called, pulling it together and peering into her new camera. She said a silent thanks to her cousin Jake for sending her on the Impulse quest. He was the one who started it all when he sent her a giant box of film cartridges in the mail last spring. Jake was fourteen and seriously into Polaroids. He had five of the vintage cameras, including a couple that were older than her parents and one that came in its own tiny suitcase and had to be opened like an accordion. Jake had taught her all kinds of stuff about the art of instant cameras. He spent several days during their annual family gathering showing her tricks for making nifty prints, how to use flashbulbs, and even how to do transfers. Lena was surprised how tricky the old "easy" cameras were. Getting a good shot was certainly harder than it seemed. Luckily, Jake knew all the secrets and had all the right accessories. And he was a great teacher.

What Jake *didn't* have was an Impulse. So when Fuji shipped him a bunch of the wrong film and then told him not to bother to send it back, he mailed the whole kit and caboodle to Lena. She had seen the offering as a challenge and had been looking for the camera to use it with since.

Until yesterday.

A fresh gust of wind came up and blew Abby's skirts dramatically, snapping Lena to attention. "Work it," she called authoritatively.

Abby posed. Lena pushed the button and her new-old camera whirred, capturing the moment. Lena listened to the cranking sound and watched as the camera spit out another flat, gray square.

"I know you don't have to shake it," Abby said, rushing up and grabbing the rectangular piece of film. "But it's more fun this way." She flapped around, goofing, and Lena glanced up and down the sidewalk. Luckily, there was no one else around to see how ridiculously they were behaving. The street was empty except for a striped cat scampering toward the bushes, and a few fallen leaves that seemed to glow in the autumn light. Half the town appeared to be away for the last weekend of summer.

"Where is everyone?" Lena wondered aloud. She took a deep breath, filling her lungs. Fall was her favorite season and she usually looked forward to it — to the changing weather, the smell of damp and rotting leaves, the start of school. But today she was feeling something else, too. . . . She just wasn't sure what to call it. She felt antsy, trapped between the two seasons and not able to enjoy either one.

I guess I'm not ready for the end of summer, she told herself. Abby had stopped her goofy flapping and was holding the film in midair. The girls watched the image slowly appear, right before their eyes. There was Abby in her wacky ensemble in front of the window at Bix, throwing a shoulder toward the camera and looking fabulous.

Except that wasn't what Lena was staring at.

There was something else going on in the photo. The window behind Abby showed Lena's reflection, aiming and squinting behind the camera. And behind her was another, fuzzier image. It looked like . . . a boy . . . watching them.

"What is *that*?" Lena asked, pulling the photo from Abby's grasp and pointing at the shape.

"It looks like a kid, but..." Somehow Lena couldn't quite bring herself to say, "Nobody was there." Even though it was true.

Snatching the picture back, Abby held it close to her face and studied it. "Could be a shadow," she said unconvincingly.

The reflected image was soft around the edges (typical Polaroid) — even Lena and the tree behind her (which *was* there for *sure*) looked blurred. The figure behind her could have been a shadow... if the real shadows in the picture weren't leaning the other way. And if the dark shape didn't have a face.

"No. Look!" Abby held the picture out a little so they could both see it. Lena could easily make out a torso, limbs, and a scowling visage. "Since when do shadows have eyes?" Abby asked quietly.

"Good point," Lena mumbled. She shivered in spite of the warming sun, and both girls looked up and down the empty street.

"I swear there was nobody there when you took the picture," Abby said. Her normally mocha-colored face looked a bit pale. "I mean, I wouldn't have been goofing like that if I thought someone was watching, you know?"

Lena knew. She would have noticed the boy, too. Just like she would have noticed the tower the day before.

"I guess we were just having too much fun to see," Abby said with a nervous smile.

"Right." Lena nodded. But she didn't believe it for a second.

CHAPTER FOUR

"Seriously. There was nobody there. I think your camera's got a weird glitch," Abby said as the girls made their way up the block.

Lena knew Abby was trying to make her feel better — make them *both* feel better — but part of her was still offended for the Impulse. She put her hand around it protectively before agreeing. "It *is* pretty old technology," she admitted.

She gave the box a little pat, an apology for doubting it, then sidestepped a fire hydrant and did a quick double step to catch up to Abby. They were only a block from Saywell's Soda Fountain and her mouth was starting to water. They'd started their walk with a plan to take a picture in front of every storefront on Second Street so they could lay them out in a row — panorama style. But since the mysterious figure had appeared, the camera had hung slack around Lena's neck. Even when Abby had mustered up a begging puppy pose in front of the pet shop, Lena hadn't risked taking another shot. She was too afraid to see what showed up in it.

"I don't know what's up with this thing," Lena said. Even though she'd been the one to offer it up, "old technology" sounded like a weak explanation for the things that were appearing in their pictures.

The only thing Lena knew for sure was that none of these rationalizations were setting her mind at ease. As she and Abby approached Saywell's, she hoped that one of their famously cold, creamy shakes would do the trick. Maybe it would be icy enough to permanently freeze the one idea she couldn't bring herself to consider: The camera was — somehow — haunted.

The bell on the drugstore door jingled as Abby pushed it open, and Lena felt a tiny bit better just hearing the familiar chime. The corner soda fountain was one of the girls' favorite places. It had been in business practically forever, a fact that showed in the worn tile floors, the dusty hanging lights, and the fading signs. Along the length of one side stood a clean but shabby lunch counter that faced the side street windows.

"Hiya, girls," Mollie, their favorite waitress, greeted from behind the counter. "Looking for a little lunch?"

"You bet," Abby replied. "It looks like we've arrived just in time." She eyed the two empty stools at the end of the counter while she held the door for Lena. Her hand pressed against one of the posters covering the glass.

Lena started to step inside and stopped. "Look." She pointed at the door. Beside Abby's hand was a huge announcement for an annual amateur photo contest. It was being held by the gallery in town and, according to the poster, the contest was celebrating its twentieth anniversary.

"Ooh, Lena. You should enter!" Abby said, nudging Lena in the rib with an elbow.

Lena shrugged, flattered. She loved to take pictures. And she'd gotten some nice shots with her digital and even her new Polaroid. Messing around with photos was definitely one of her favorite things to do. But carrying a camera around and trying to snap something cool was one thing. Putting pictures in a contest where serious photographers would be competing was quite another. Besides, at the moment her new hobby had her a little spooked.

Shrugging off Abby's suggestion, Lena hurried her friend along to the stools at the end of the counter, which happened to have the best view. "What are you getting?" she asked, purposely changing the subject.

"BLT and a mint-chip shake," Abby replied, her dark eyes twinkling. "What else would I get?"

No sooner were the girls seated than Mollie was there to take their order. "The usual today, girls?" she asked.

Lena nodded. "And a basket of fries to share."

Mollie grinned and filled a coffee mug a couple of seats down before putting their order in.

"All right, let's see how we're doing," Abby said, holding out her hand for the morning's photos. Lena gave her the small stack and Abby laid them out in a row, leaving out the creepy photo with the boy.

"Wow, Lena!" she crowed. "These are really good!"

Lena looked down at the photos and blushed. There was a lot of variety, a little blur, and some great composition.

"You *have* to enter that contest," Abby encouraged. She thumped one of the squares. "I mean, I have never seen anyone who could make a Polaroid look this awesome."

Lena scrunched her nose at the compliment. The Polaroids were coming out nicely, she had to admit. They had a muted quality that made them sort of timeless. Or maybe that was just the camera. Or Abby's retro style. Whatever it was, it was working. The shots drew attention.

"Did you take those, Lena?" Mollie asked as she set their shakes down behind the row of photos. "They're terrific."

"She totally did," Abby confirmed, nodding emphatically. "And she really *should* enter the photo contest, don't you think?"

"Sure thing," Mollie said, sticking her pencil behind her ear and turning to slice up a homemade berry pie.

"Come on, Lena. You know you want to."

Lena sipped her shake. She thought maybe she

did want to, but wasn't totally sure. Attention made her feel a little squirmy. And she was already feeling a little . . . weird.

"I wouldn't stand a chance," Lena said. "Besides, taking photos is just for fun." Or was supposed to be.

"Hey, how come you're not hogging the fries?" Abby asked when they were done with their sandwiches but still sipping milk shakes.

Lena looked at the nearly full basket. "Not that hungry, I guess." She shrugged and took another sip. The Impulse pressed up against her ribs as she leaned toward the counter. She hadn't taken it off to eat.

"Let's head out, then." Abby slid off her stool and left a few bills on the counter for a tip while Lena gathered the pics. "We still have a few blocks to cover, and *Vanity Fair* is going to be clamoring to get their hands on your proofs."

"Yes, of course. How else will they be able to pick a cover?" Lena joked back. She shoved open the door to Saywell's and tried to push the strange thoughts out of her mind. The boy and the tower were just optical tricks, nothing to worry about. She had her new-old camera — the one she had hunted for for months — and everything was right with the world. Really.

Before leaving Saywell's storefront, Abby stood in front of the red-and-white sign and dabbed a napkin to the corner of her mouth exaggeratedly.

"Nice one!" Lena caught the shot, then paused by a trash can to change film cartridges while Abby hurried ahead to scout out the next perfect site.

With the camera reloaded, Lena skipped past the door to Don's Pawnshop — and for good reason. There wasn't much to see there. A few years earlier, Lena and Abby had gone into Don's thinking it might be a fun place to unleash their thrift savvy and sniff out bargains. It had only taken a second to smell the jacked-up prices and catch a whiff of the store's "no haggle" policy. Don, or whoever it was who ran the place, overpriced everything and demanded full sticker. Not only that, the owners were totally paranoid about shoplifting, so there were video cameras everywhere and the merchandise was either behind glass or up on high shelves, creating a very unwelcoming feeling all around. Luckily, it didn't really matter, since the store was mostly stocked with jewelry, silver, and musical instruments — nothing that Lena and Abby were into.

"Come on, girl!" Abby called from two doors down. She was in front of the hardware store, squatting in a shiny red wheelbarrow. Lena grinned and stepped up her pace so she'd get there before Abby was caught riding the merchandise.

Then something made her turn back. She lifted the Impulse to her face and pointed it at the pawnshop window. She felt a little like a puppet, without control of her limbs, just as she had in the car the day before. Without intending to, she snapped a shot of the dusty display of jewels in the window.

Weirdness.

Why in the world would she want a picture of the Don's Pawnshop window? Shaking her head in disbelief, she pulled the picture out of the bottom of the camera and shoved it in her bag. It was sure to be a waste of film.

"Lena, come on!" Abby called from up ahead.

Dropping the camera to her side, Lena hurried to catch up to her friend. She was able to get two wheelbarrow shots before the scowling owner waved them on.

Abby climbed out of the shiny garden transport with a mischievous smile. "Should we get one on the mini-tractor?" she whispered.

Lena laughed and glanced at the shop owner. "I'm not sure if we should push our —"

"Whoa. Check that out!" Abby stopped dusting off her skirt long enough to point at a slowly passing truck. The formerly blue pickup was covered with a zillion bottle caps, glued to the outside like a mosaic. "That's not something you see every day."

Lena instinctively lifted the camera and snapped a photo just before the truck rounded a corner and rumbled out of sight. "Cool," Lena breathed, happy to have gotten the picture. For such an old camera, the Impulse was pretty responsive.

The pair moved more slowly now, thanks to milk shakes and the hour. Lena stifled a yawn. Abby rubbed the merit badges sewn to the stomach of her shirt. "I'm stuffed," she said. "I think I might need a nap."

A nap sounded good to Lena, too. She hadn't slept very well the night before. She kept waking up and checking to make sure the Impulse was still on her desk. She yawned again, feeling her lids growing heavier as she watched the picture in her hand develop. When the image of the truck finally appeared, her eyes snapped open wide.

It had happened again. The boy-shadow was there — a little clearer this time — sitting in the back of the truck, staring out at them. Even in the grainy photo, the eyes in the dark face were intense and spooky. One ghostly hand hung over the tailgate of the truck, balled into a tight fist.

"Abby . . ." Lena said. She didn't need to say more. In an instant her friend was by her side, peering at the photo.

"Holy moley," Abby breathed. "He's back."

Lena looked around anxiously. She had a feeling he'd never left.

CHAPTER FIVE

Lena rolled over. She kicked off the sheet — her last remaining cover — and flipped her pillow to the cool side. She was hot, and without looking she knew there was no possible way the big hand on her alarm clock had made it more than halfway around the dial. It was just past one A.M. and she hadn't gotten a lick of sleep.

She blamed the weather. By the time the girls got back from their photo session, the blazing sun had scared off the autumn breeze, and summer had reasserted its sticky hold. Lena's room was way too warm for sleeping. For a moment she toyed with the idea of turning on the light and trying to read. If she picked the right book — a really, really boring one — she might be able to knock herself out in a couple of pages. But just the thought of light in the dark room made her feel hotter, and she didn't think she could get any hotter without melting.

She flipped her pillow again and settled into it with a sigh. She tuned out every thought, or at least tried to, and focused on the *tick, tick, tick* of the clock. After what felt like another three hours, she finally fell asleep.

Even asleep, Lena couldn't get any real rest. The moment her breathing grew regular she felt herself running down long rows of strawberries. She had no idea why she was running, she only knew she had to. She raced down an endless row, her heart thumping in her chest. She was out of breath. But there was someone behind her — someone she desperately wanted to avoid. Or perhaps something in front of her — something she desperately wanted to see.

Her feet thudded on the ground over and over until she wasn't sure if she was forcing them to keep moving or if they were forcing her. Then, all at once, the rows of berries gave way to something new.

She wasn't running any longer. She was climbing. Up, up, and up she went, getting higher and higher. The rungs of the ladder were slanted, the gaps uncomfortably wide. She hoisted herself step-by-step, panting with the effort. Her legs burned. She could barely see. All around was fog, or haze, or blur. She ignored whatever it was and kept climbing. She had to get to the top. . . .

Suddenly, the climbing was over. She had arrived, apparently, and was seated on a small shelf. She knew she had to be up really high, but she couldn't see through the thick white mist that surrounded her.

Lifting the camera from around her neck (had it been there a moment before?), Lena held it in front of her face. Her vision cleared, but what she saw made her want to close her eyes. She was several stories above the strawberry field, not running, not climbing, not sitting. She was falling. Falling fast.

Lena woke with her heart pounding and her back damp with sweat. Looking around her darkened room, she knew she'd been dreaming. She wasn't falling — she was safe and sound in bed. Her clock read 4:45. The camera was beside it, the viewfinder looking at her like a mechanical cyclops.

She changed her tank top, flipped her pillow (again!), and slipped back into bed. Closing her eyes, she tried to change the movie playing over in her

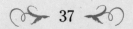

mind, remind herself it was just a dream. But even awake and solidly in her bed, she felt as though she were falling. . . .

As soon as the sun was up, Lena was, too. She jumped out of bed, grabbed a frayed-hem denim skirt out of her closet, and riffled through her dresser. The pale green T-shirt that Abby had customized for her seemed as good a choice as any, and she pulled it on before slipping the Impulse strap over her head. As soon as the camera was hanging at her side, she felt dressed. A quick comb-through of her strawberry-blond hair and she was on her way.

From the top of the stairs she could smell simmering peaches. Her dad had started canning early to beat the heat — obviously a losing battle. Just walking into the kitchen made Lena break into a sweat.

"Mmm." Mr. Giff mumbled a greeting through a bite of toast covered in warm, foamy jam skimmings. "Wanf smmm?" he asked with his mouth full.

It did smell good, but Lena shook her head. Her

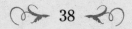

stomach was jumping all over the place. She wanted to talk to Abby.

"I'm heading over to Abby's for breakfast," Lena fibbed, slipping her messenger bag over her head and making her getaway before her dad asked for help. "Happy canning." She waved, and was out the door.

The urge to run the three blocks to Abby's house was beaten down by temperature and tiredness. Lena walked as quickly as she could without breaking a sweat, trying not to let the nightmare replay in her head.

Abby was sprawled on a futon on the screened-in porch of her house on Bixby Street, wearing old-man boxer shorts and a tank top. Her skinny brown arms and legs were flung out wide, as if they were afraid to touch anything. She was awake, but barely. When she saw Lena, she held out her hand like a star trying to block photographers.

"Stop with the paparazzi!" she mumbled. "It's too early for pictures."

Lena tried to laugh at the joke, but all she managed was a feeble smile. It *was* too early for pictures. She didn't even know why she'd worn the camera.

Well, actually, she sort of did. Ever since she'd bought the Impulse, not wearing it felt really weird. Whenever she took it off, an anxious feeling came over her, like something terrible was going to happen. And that was what she wanted to talk to Abby about.

"I think I'm being haunted," she blurted.

In an instant Abby was wide-awake. She sat up and swung her long legs over the edge of the futon. Her dark eyes looked worried. "You think you're being what?"

"Haunted," Lena repeated in a hoarse whisper. Now that she'd said the words, she suddenly felt a little woozy. She steadied herself against the pillar at the top of the stairs. "You know, by that boy," she went on. "And the tower. The things that are showing up." Lena took a deep breath, several slow steps, and climbed into the hammock that was strung across a corner of the Starlings' porch. "I think the camera is haunted, or like, a medium — one of those things ghosts use to communicate," she finished. Wow. She wasn't really planning on saying all of that — it just kind of came out. *When did I decide I was being haunted?* she wondered with a shudder.

Lena pulled the tower picture, the one that had

started it all, out of her bag and stared at it for a long time. Abby sighed, got to her feet, and worked her way into the hammock beside her so the two of them could look at it together.

The hammock swung slowly back and forth, the fabric creaking on the hooks that held it. Lena heaved a sigh. It was a bit of a relief to have put her spooky suspicions into words, and another relief that Abby hadn't laughed. But if what she said was true, things would undoubtedly get a lot worse before they got better . . . if they got better at all.

"You can't get that tower out of your head, can you?" Abby finally asked. "I wish I had seen it. Or not seen it. Or whatever."

"I wish you had seen it, too." Lena pressed her lips together. "Or that I hadn't. Actually, I just wish I could stop thinking about it, or dreaming about it. . . ."

"Dreaming about it?" Abby echoed.

Lena nodded. "And not good dreams."

"Ew. Nightmares." Abby's eyes looked genuinely worried now. She put her hand on Lena's shoulder for an instant, then took it away to pick up one of the photos. "Hey . . ." Abby pulled the picture closer to her face. "This is weird."

The whole thing is weird, Lena thought. But she leaned in to see what her friend was pointing at.

Abby's blue-painted fingernail was hovering over the letters on the water tower in the photo. "The town is 'Phelps,' right?"

Lena nodded and looked closer, immediately seeing what Abby was talking about.

"Check it out. There are only four of the letters of the town's name in this picture: *h, e, l,* and *p*. And that spells . . ."

"Help," Lena finished. "Maybe the shadow needs our help," she added quietly. "Maybe there's something about that tower that he wants us to know."

The air in the screened-in porch felt closer and hotter than ever. Gray clouds were gathering, throwing a blanket on the sky.

The creepy feeling Lena had been trying to shake settled hard around her shoulders. She wished it weren't so muggy. She wished she could crawl into Abby's abandoned bed. She wished she could hide under the covers for eternity.

"Well, I guess that's better than *beware,*" Abby breathed.

Lena laughed nervously. She supposed Abby had a point. So far it didn't seem like the boy wanted to hurt her. But he was super-creepy in the pictures, and last night's nightmare was terrifying.

Lena could feel her heart thudding in her chest. She was trying not to panic, but . . .

"We need some answers," Abby said after studying Lena's troubled face. She grabbed Lena by the hand and pulled her through the screen door and into the den, which was thankfully cooler than outside. Abby pulled an extra chair up to the desk and gently pushed Lena into it. "Time for a little research," she announced as she slid into her own chair and switched on the family computer.

Lena smiled, grateful for her friend's action-taking nature. They waited while the machine hummed to life, then did a Google search for "Phelps water tower."

"Not Phelps County in Nebraska, though," Abby said with a chuckle, glancing through the listings that came up.

Lena couldn't laugh. She was still trying to wrap her head around the fact that she was being haunted.

"Or Georgia," Abby added, scrolling down and clicking on the only entry that looked like it might apply — a brief article about Malcolm Phelps, the founder of Phelps, New Jersey. He'd had the tower built in 1919.

"Well, at least I know that the dang thing actually exists," Lena breathed, feeling a tiny bit relieved. "Or existed . . ."

Abby tried a few more searches, but couldn't find anything to confirm whether the tower still stood or not.

"That's the Internet for you, totally incomplete," Lena declared, parroting her father, who was a high school teacher. It was odd, because she wasn't sure if she wanted the tower to be there. On the one hand, it would mean that the camera had captured reality (a welcome change). On the other, how could she have missed something so huge and obvious?

Abby was about to start a new search when the screen went dark. "Uh-oh," she said. "I think I crashed it." She tried to reboot. Nothing. Lena checked the plugs. Everything looked fine, but the computer seemed dead.

"This thing is practically new," Abby said, giving the monitor a gentle whack. "It's never done anything like this before."

Lena got to her feet, and the Polaroid knocked lightly against the edge of the desk. She glanced down, momentarily wondering if the camera had anything to do with the computer crash.

"It's cool," Abby reassured her. "My mom is a whiz with this stuff. She'll get it up and running in no time. And we need to get out of here, anyway. You look like you've seen a gho —" She stopped herself. "Well, you've looked better," she corrected.

Abby got up and started to put on her shoes before she noticed she was still wearing her pajamas. "Wait here," she told her friend. "I don't want to ruin my reputation as a fashionista. . . ."

After Abby disappeared upstairs, Lena pulled out the picture of the Phelps tower. It looked just like the one they'd seen on the Internet. Confirmation. Right? "Are you there?" she whispered to the photo. A hot breeze coming through the screen door was the only answer she got.

Abby returned dressed in a cute skirt and sandals and scarfing down a bagel. "I'm guessing there's no way we can talk your dad into a return trip to Phelps?" she half asked. "That would be the easiest way to go back and see what's really there."

Lena shook her head. Her dad was in full jam production, so unless he ran out of fruit, it wasn't even worth asking him to step away from the stove.

He would simmer fruit and jars and measure sugar and pectin all day. By evening the kitchen would be filled with jam and they'd have pizza for dinner.

"And I'm also guessing you won't sleep again until you have proof that tower is really there?" Abby raised a brow.

Lena grimaced. Right again. She just had to know if the tower in her photo had been there when she snapped the shot . . . or not. If she knew that, she might be able to unravel the mystery of the boy.

"Okay. Then we need to go somewhere where we can do some real research," Abby concluded. And without waiting for an answer, she shoved the last bite of bagel into her mouth and grabbed Lena by the hand.

CHAPTER SIX

Even though Abby didn't say so, Lena knew exactly where they were going. It was no secret that Abby loved the town library almost as much as a flea market, and Lena was a big fan, too. The ancient stone building was large and grand and smelled of books. And, best of all, it was air-conditioned.

"Information desk, here we come," Abby announced as Lena took a picture of her walking through the front door. "I hope that grumpy old guy with the crazy beard isn't working today. . . ."

Luckily, Captain Whiskers wasn't at the desk. A bookish but friendly-looking woman with red hair and reading glasses was sitting behind it instead. "We're looking for information on the Phelps water tower," Abby said, getting right to the point.

The woman looked up from the stack of books she was checking in and smiled. "Phelps water tower?" she repeated. "You mean the one that was torn down?"

Lena nearly choked on her tongue. *How easy was that?!* she thought. A single sentence gave her confirmation that the giant tower 1) had existed and 2) had been demolished. "Yes," she cried, a little more emphatically than she meant to. "That's the one." Then, just as fast, her next thought erased the relief she'd felt. If it had been torn down, what was it doing in her picture?

"Do you happen to know *when* they tore it down?" Abby asked. She was great at details. And actually, if the tower had been torn down yesterday then it *could* have still been there in the picture.

"Hmmmm," the librarian said thoughtfully. "I'm not sure, but I think it was sometime in the late nineties. I remember it being kind of a big deal at the time . . . lots of people protested the demolition. It was in the paper for weeks."

"Well. There you go." Abby clucked her tongue. "Thanks a lot for your —" Lena grabbed her friend's arm to keep her from walking away.

"Is there any way we can search those old

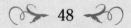

newspapers?" Lena asked. "You know, read some of the articles you mentioned?"

"Certainly," the librarian replied with a smile. "I can set you up with some rolls of microfilm and you can search to your heart's content. It might take a while to find the right dates, but if you're feeling patient I'm sure you'll find them." The librarian got to her feet and the girls followed her toward the back of the building.

Lena wasn't feeling particularly patient — more like the opposite. The gears were spinning wildly in her mind. Every answer seemed to lead to a new question. If the tower wasn't there anymore but it showed up in the picture, what about the boy?

"What exactly are we looking for?" Abby whispered as they walked past long, tall rows of neatly shelved books.

"I don't know yet," Lena replied. She hoped she'd know when she saw it.

The librarian stepped inside a quiet room filled with flat files and several machines. "These cabinets hold all the *Narrowsburg Bugler*s printed since the paper was first published in 1908," she said, donning her reading glasses so she could make out the tiny labels on the drawers. She opened one near the bottom. "I would start with late spring of 1997 — that should be far back enough — and work your way forward."

"Great, thanks," Abby said. She pulled open a drawer and ran a finger along the boxes of rolled film. Clearly her tenacity was kicking in. Lena eyed the rows and rows (and rows) of microfilm and felt her heart sink. This was going to be like finding a needle in a haystack.

"Here we go. June 1, 1997," Abby said, pulling the roll out of the drawer. Then she reached back in and grabbed several more boxes. "Can you get the 1999s?" she asked, nearly dropping a bunch of film.

Lena caught two rolls before they fell to the floor, plucked the last three from the drawer, and followed her best friend to the microfilm machines. Abby started to set herself up on one. There was another beside her, but Lena hesitated.

"I know it would be faster if we each took a machine, but I kind of want to look together," Lena said.

Abby slid the film into the machine. "Oookaaaay," she said, drawing the word out and asking her friend without actually asking: *Are you all right?*

"I'm just a little weirded out is all," Lena replied. Her sleepless night was catching up with her — her head felt like it was packed with cotton.

Lena pulled a chair up beside Abby's and together they watched newspaper headlines and articles whiz by on the screen in front of them.

After what seemed like an hour, but was probably six minutes, Abby paused on an ad for ultra-hold mousse. "Check out that hairdo," she said, pointing at the image on the screen. The woman in the picture had a puffy bob and bangs with a life of their own — they hovered about two inches above her eyebrows.

"Niiice," Lena replied halfheartedly. Even though she was the reason they were searching for clues, she felt herself growing more and more anxious. At the moment, she just wanted to get out of there! Lena let out a long breath, adjusted the Impulse at her side, and tried to stop fidgeting.

Abby finished her second roll of microfilm and slid the end of a third into the machine. The images whirred along in a seemingly endless blur. "I'm not finding anything," Abby confessed after a while. "You want to take a shot?"

Lena glanced out the window. A group of kids

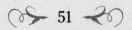

was shrieking, running through a sprinkler. Enjoying the heat.

"Hello? Lena?" Abby called.

"Sorry," Lena apologized, shaking her head. Poor Abby was doing all the work while she was zoning out. She reached for the next box of microfilm and saw it had been unrolled and lay in coils all over the table beside her. Had she done that? She looked down at her hands, folded in her lap. She didn't remember moving them.

Lena shivered. "Actually, I don't want to look anymore," she said. "This is getting us nowhere. Summer is almost over, and what are we doing? Reading old newspapers! Let's get out of here."

Abby raised an eyebrow at her friend and opened her mouth to say something, then closed it instead. Without another word she pushed a lever, rewound the film, pulled it off the machine, and slipped it back into the box.

Lena was grateful not to have to explain why she wanted to leave. "Thanks," she said as she got to her feet, gathering up the roll of spilled film. She collected the others, dropped two, and started cramming them back into the file cabinet.

"Whoa there, girl," Abby said, taking the remaining film out of her friend's hands. "They go in rows. . . ."

Lena handed the boxes over. "I just want to have a little fun," she said, trying to sound more light-hearted than she felt. "We have exactly two days before school starts." Lena pulled the strap away from where it was sticking to her neck.

"I'm all for fun," Abby agreed, straightening the final rolls in the cabinet before sliding it closed.

"Can I take the camera for a while?" Abby asked when they got outside. "You know, to give you a little break?" She started to lift it off Lena's head.

Lena instinctively grabbed the strap, holding it around her neck.

Abby looked totally serious for a second, then laughed. "I just want to try it out," she cajoled. "I haven't even had a chance to click the shutter!"

Lena felt ridiculous holding on to the strap, so she let go and lifted the camera over her head. But her hands were a little shaky as she handed it to Abby. And just as Abby put the Impulse around her own neck, a giant gust of wind kicked up, blowing a pile of leaves around them like a tiny tornado.

Then, as quickly as the wind had appeared, it was gone.

Freaky, Lena thought.

"Gross!" Abby said, spitting bits of dry foliage out of her mouth. "How bad is my hair?" she asked, leaning down so Lena could evaluate.

Lena inspected the tight braids and pulled out a few twigs and bits of leaf. "Not too terrible," she said. "Mine?"

"Reasonable," Abby replied, returning the leaf-removal favor. "Let's get the bikes."

Minutes later the girls were rolling down Main Street. Abby cruised slowly along in front of Lena, window-shopping and stopping to take a few shots with the camera. Lena tried not to crash into her and to ignore the worrying fear that was growing in the pit of her stomach. First the computer. Then the weird, blowing leaves. What next?

Abby rolled to a stop in front of their favorite yogurt shop, parking her bike near the curb. "Feel like a cup of frozen happiness?" she asked with a grin.

Lena knew better than to say no. "Love one," she lied.

"My treat," Abby said, hopping off her bike. She disappeared into the store and came back with two cups of light orange swirls. The two girls sat down on a little bench in front of the store.

Abby took a giant frozen bite. "I love peach season," she said through her mouthful.

Lena took a bite and tried to let the sweetness seep in. It was delicious. "Not as much as my dad," she said with a laugh. "He was in the kitchen at dawn."

"Sounds good to me," Abby said. "His jam is amazing. Did you know he offered to teach me? Maybe we should head back. It's only eleven o'clock."

"Go back to that hot kitchen?" Lena squinted in disgust. "Are you crazy?" She set down her yogurt and held out her hand. "Can I have the camera? I want to take a shot." She could already picture the close-up of the cup and spoon through the viewfinder.

Abby gave her a look, but lifted the strap over her head.

Lena took the camera. It felt really good to have it back in her hands, as if she'd been without it for days instead of a mere fifteen minutes. She found the shot of the spoon in the yogurt cup through the viewfinder and pressed the button, but nothing came out. "You used up the film!" she protested, shooting Abby a pretend dirty look.

Abby scraped the bottom of her yogurt cup with her spoon and looked nonplussed. "We both know you have another package in your bag, and five hundred more at home," she replied smoothly.

Lena smirked, feeling normal for the first time that day. "Thank you, Jake!" she cried.

The girls finished their treats in silence, climbed back on their bikes, and rode the rest of the way down Main Street. Lena struggled to keep a hold on her easy mood, but could feel it slipping away.

Just before rounding the corner onto Fourth, Abby screeched to a halt, leaving black tire marks on the cement.

"A little warning might be nice!" Lena yelped, quickly steering to the left to avoid a crash. Without replying, Abby propped her bike next to a building and slipped inside.

"The girl's gone loco," Lena said to herself. She shook her head when she saw where Abby was going, then locked the bikes and followed her friend into the art gallery. "Didn't I tell her I don't want to enter the photo contest?" she complained to no one in particular.

The gallery was cool and quiet inside, with high ceilings and exposed beams. The floorboards creaked as Lena caught up to her friend in the back of the big, open room. Abby was standing in front of a wall hung with a long row of pictures.

"What gives?" Lena asked, feeling a little grumpy about her friend's unannounced stop.

"I just felt like stopping," Abby said. "Here, I got this for you." She shoved an entry form into Lena's hand and turned her attention back to the wall of photos. "These are all the contest winners."

Lena knew from experience (and from watching her best friend drive hard bargains) that Abby didn't take no for an answer. Most of the time this was totally fine, and even entertaining. But when Abby's pushiness was directed *at* her, it could be totally annoying. She crumpled the form into a tight ball and glanced up at the winning images in spite of herself. Within five seconds she was hooked.

The shots varied widely — there were images of

everything from a super-close-up of a happy dog's tongue to a dewy meadow at sunrise, to a weirdly disturbing image of a place setting missing its spoon.

Every picture told a story, which was exactly what Lena loved about photographs. She loved how a moment captured in the blink of the shutter could say so much more than seemed possible.

Lena and Abby lingered over the back wall. All of the shots were great. But time and again Lena kept coming back to one picture — the black-and-white silverware shot. Simple as it was, it was oddly captivating. It looked like it had been taken at a diner — possibly even Saywell's. Lena liked the way the curved coffee stain marked the spot where the spoon should have been. It had a lonely quality.

"Check it out," Abby said, pointing at two placards beneath the photos. "Some guy named Robbie Henson won twice in a row."

Sure enough, the photos were credited with the same name. One was a shot of three sets of toes dangling off a dock just above the water — a man, woman, and child obviously enjoying summer. The other was the napkin-coffee-stain image Lena had just been staring at.

"The images are so different," Abby said thoughtfully. "You'd never guess they were taken by the same person."

Lena discreetly uncrumpled the entry form. She flattened it and pushed it into her messenger bag. It was amazing how one picture could completely change the way you saw things.

CHAPTER SEVEN

The girls stood silently in front of the photos for several minutes. "Just think," Abby said, turning toward Lena. "Your name could be up here, too!"

Lena rolled her eyes. Thinking about entering was one thing. Planning on winning was quite another. "Let's just take it one step at a time," she replied. Abby was the queen of putting the cart before the horse.

"The seed has been planted," Abby said with a knowing smile. She turned toward the door.

"You're such a pest," Lena teased, lightly pinching her on the arm and following behind. Abby was just reaching for the door handle when a crash echoed from the back of the room.

Lena knew what had happened before she turned

to look. One of the pictures had fallen off the wall. But which one? Glancing back, she felt her stomach tighten. It was the coffee stain photo she'd just been admiring. The glass in the frame had shattered, and Lena felt her nerves splinter right along with it.

"Goodness!" came a voice as a tall, salt-and-pepper–haired man appeared and rushed to the back wall of the gallery. "What happened here?" he asked the air.

The girls watched as he stooped to examine the photo and lean it carefully against the wall. Then he disappeared again, presumably to get a broom.

"Let's go," Abby whispered.

Lena thought maybe they should stay, but since they weren't anywhere near the photo when it fell they obviously weren't responsible, and the man clearly had the situation under control. Nodding, she followed her friend back into the heat.

The girls unlocked their bikes and rode side by side up Fourth Street. Neither of them spoke. Lena tried to think happy thoughts, but the spooky mood from earlier in the day was oozing back in, like horror movie slime.

"Hey," Abby suddenly said, breaking the silence and looking like she'd just had a brain wave. "We should have a sleepover tonight. Tomorrow's the last free day before school starts, so our parents can't say no."

Lena hesitated. They had sleepovers all the time, of course. But Lena knew she wouldn't be very good company. Plus, she had no interest in staying up late. She really just wanted to sleep.

"Come on. We have to live a little before it's back to the grind," Abby urged.

"Sounds good," Lena finally replied. It didn't really, but it did sound better than staying home alone — her parents had plans to go out.

"Perfect. I'll just gather a few things, get the all-clear from the 'rents, and see you back at your place." Abby waved and split off down her own street.

"Perfect," Lena echoed. But she felt far from it.

When Abby showed up at the Giffs' a few hours later, Lena was still in a fog.

"Don't you ever take that thing off?" Abby wrinkled her nose and pointed at the Impulse as she breezed into the living room. She dropped her bag and her backside on the couch.

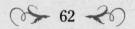

"What thing?" Lena asked. She glanced down and saw that the camera was still hanging around her neck. She hadn't even realized it was there, that she'd been wandering around the house with it all afternoon. "I was just about to grab a shot of my dad's jam," she lied. "You should see it."

Abby followed Lena into the kitchen, where rows of gleaming jam-filled jars lined the counters, waiting for labels. The last batch was still hot, the jars sitting upside down to prevent bacteria from growing.

"Come to admire my handiwork?" Mr. Giff asked, sauntering into the kitchen dressed for a night out and wearing a wide smile. "Hello, my beauties," he greeted his jam, patting the bottom of a hot jar.

Lena rolled her eyes and decided not to point out that he was going to be *eating* his little beauties in the very near future.

Mr. Giff dropped some cash on the counter for pizza and turned back to the girls. "I didn't see you in jam class today, Abby. You really should come help me and learn some of my tricks. I don't offer my jam-making secrets to just anyone, you know." His eyes twinkled.

"I totally want to make jam with you, Mr. G. We

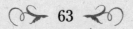

just got, uh, a little distracted today." She shot Lena a look.

Lena felt a twinge of guilt. Her best friend had spent most of the day trying to help her unravel the Impulse mystery. She vowed that tonight would be different. Tonight she was going to have fun.

She trained the camera's eye on her father and one of his beauties. "Smile, Dad," she directed. Shifting the camera to the left, she fit as many jars into the shot as she could and pushed the button. The camera whirred.

"Next time, Mr. G.," Abby vowed. "Next time we are going to have a stellar jam session." She smiled and ran her finger along the gleaming line of jars.

Mr. Giff handed the jar he was holding to Abby. "This one's for you. As for our lesson, I wish I had time tomorrow. There's a whole flat of peaches on the porch I didn't even get to." He shook his head dramatically. "But I have a meeting, so this lot will have to get us through."

Lena looked at the rows and rows of jars. It was definitely enough to get them through the winter, plus extras to give away to friends. Not to mention the two cases of strawberry jam in the pantry. But according to her dad, you couldn't have too much jam.

"What a waste," Mr. Giff murmured. "And I'm a little short this year, too."

"Don't worry, Dad," Lena said, patting her father on the back. "I've heard of this crazy thing you can do with peaches. It's called *eating* them."

"Smart aleck," Mr. Giff harrumphed. He checked his watch and called out to Lena's mother.

"What time did you say the movie started?" Mrs. Giff appeared in the kitchen in the nick of time. She looked at the girls and lifted her eyebrows. "Is he still whining about the jam?" she asked.

They didn't have to answer.

"Don't worry, I'll get him out of here," Mrs. Giff joked, and tried to tug her husband toward the door. "The man needs distraction."

POP! A small explosion echoed in the kitchen.

"What the —" Lena turned and her mouth dropped open. One of the upside-down jars had popped its lid and was oozing sticky peach goo all over the counter. *POP!* Another one opened up.

"What's going on?" Mrs. Giff asked.

"I don't know! I don't know!" Mr. Giff wailed. "I was just going to flip them over. Everything seemed fine, and now . . ."

65

A third jar popped, and peach jam flowed out the bottom like lava.

"Honey, we have to go," Mrs. Giff called her husband from the hallway. "We'll miss the movie."

"But . . ." Mr. Giff looked from the door to the jam and back.

"Don't worry, Dad. We'll clean it up." Lena wasn't sure she'd ever seen her father so distraught.

"I made sure everything was boiling hot. I used the same pectin. I . . ." Mr. Giff walked slowly out of the kitchen talking to himself, going over each step and wondering what had gone wrong. "I suppose the lids might be defective. . . ."

Or something else, Lena thought.

"Man. Your dad was a mess," Abby said after the door was closed and locked behind Lena's parents.

"Yeah. So's the counter," Lena pointed out. The sticky peach ooze was spreading out under the jars, sealing them to the granite. Suddenly, Lena was regretting her offer to clean up.

"Okay. You wash, I'll dry," Abby said, taking charge.

Lena turned on the hot water, added soap, and

began to carefully wash the bottoms of the still-sealed jars. The Impulse clunked awkwardly against the counter every time she reached for another jar.

"Why don't you take that thing off?" Abby asked.

Lena felt a flash of annoyance. One minute she wanted her to enter the photo contest, and the next she was telling her to ditch the camera. . . .

The Impulse thunked against the lip of the sink again, this time coming dangerously close to getting wet. Abby had a point, Lena realized, and she was being ridiculous. Reaching up, she removed the strap and set the camera on the counter nearby. There. That was better.

Or was it? In an instant her anxiousness was back, and Lena could feel herself starting to rush through the cleanup. She had to get it done! She finished the washing, then grabbed the dried jars off the counter and carried them into the pantry.

"There, that's done," she declared as she set the final jar in its place. She was about to snatch up the camera when Abby suddenly jumped into her path, a suspiciously sly grin on her face.

Oh no, Lena thought. *What now?*

CHAPTER EIGHT

"How many times have you watched your dad make jam?" Abby asked, arching an eyebrow.

"About a gazillion," Lena answered. She tried to duck around Abby's arm to grab the Impulse off the counter, but Abby shifted again — right into the center of her path.

"So, you know how to do it, right?" Abby prodded.

Something in her tone made Lena stop trying to get around her and look into her face instead. "Yeaah . . ." she said slowly.

"So, I bet we could make a batch ourselves," Abby concluded. "To help him out." A slow smile crept across her face. Any trace of a smile disappeared from Lena's.

As if we aren't already in hot water, Lena thought. But Lena had been cooking and baking in their kitchen since she was ten, and once Abby had an idea in her head there was no stopping her. Lena had seen Abby's determination lead to some amazing successes, like first place at the science fair in fourth grade, and the bake sale sellout earlier this summer. But she had also been witness to some spectacular failures, such as (but not limited to) the front yard ice-skating rink catastrophe and the doggie day-care disaster. With the way things had been going lately, she was pretty sure that the great jam session would fall into the "failure" category.

Forty minutes later, the girls were wrist-deep in peach peeling and pulping. Lena picked up a blanched yellow ball and easily peeled the skin away. She split the peach in half with her fingers, let the peach halves fall into a giant bowl of already-peeled peaches, and dropped the peel and the pit into the compost tub.

"That's peach number five hundred and sixty-two," she groused.

"Oh, come on, this is fun," Abby corrected as she dumped a giant pile of peach chunks into a flat-bottomed dish for mashing. "And besides, I'm already pulping."

It was true. With both girls working they were making good time.

Abby finished her cutting and walked over to the sink, using her elbow to turn on the faucet. Her peachy hands reminded Lena of scrubbed-up doctors, only it was peach juice instead of disinfectant. What they really needed were spikes on the tips of their fingers. Peeling peaches was slippery business.

"You get back here!" Lena called as a peach slid out of her fingers and onto the floor. It hit the tile with a *sploosh*, skidded across the kitchen, and wedged itself under the fridge.

Abby retrieved it and rinsed it in the sink. "Nobody has to know," she said with a giggle as she finished washing up. They were finally ready to make jam.

Lena measured several cups of peach pulp into a big pot and set it on the stove. Behind her, Abby excitedly ripped open a box of pectin.

"So, how much of this stuff do I put in?" Abby asked, gazing into the pot of peach pulp. "Mmm, smells good already."

"Check the directions," Lena said. "They're in the box."

Abby pulled out the little paper envelope and peered into the cardboard container. "No directions here," she said, turning the box upside down and giving it a little shake to demonstrate.

Lena let out a little groan. No directions? Bummer. How many times had her dad told her that eyeballing quantities was for professional jam-makers only, and risky no matter what?

About a hundred thousand . . .

Abby ripped open the paper envelope of thickener. It came loose with a jolt, and white powder rained down on the edge of the counter.

Lena looked into the pot. "I've got five cups of pulp," she said. "So I'm pretty sure we put in the whole thing." She tried to picture her dad doing this. "Maybe two," she mumbled. Pectin made the jam thicken, and she wanted it to hurry up and work so they could get out of there. She felt sticky all over. But there was something she was forgetting. . . . Her eyes drifted to the Impulse, waiting patiently on the counter.

Abby poured in a second packet of pectin. "There. What now?"

"Turn the stove on pretty high. We need it to boil. . . ." *Oh no!* Lena thought. It wasn't just the jam that was supposed to boil. The jars were supposed to be boiled, too!

Thank goodness Dad doesn't process the jam in a boiling water bath like most jam-makers do, Lena thought, chewing a nail. *That would be a double whammy!*

"We were supposed to boil the jars!" she exclaimed.

Pushing the Impulse aside, the girls scrambled to get eight empty jam jars into a pot and cover them with water. The filled pot was so heavy, it took them both to put it on the stove. The water sloshed, soaking Lena's sleeve.

Lena stirred the just-started-to-boil peach mixture on the stove, then added the sugar and boiled it for a minute before turning it down. It was looking gloppy, and not as bright as her dad's usually did. Lena didn't have the heart to tell Abby her dad's secret to great jam: quick cooking time. This was not going to be her dad's jam.

"So . . . what are we going to do while we wait?" Abby asked. She pulled herself up on the counter, her shoes making a sticky noise when they left the floor.

Lena lifted the camera. She licked her thumb and wiped off a shiny blob of peach. Abby wrinkled her nose. She'd obviously had enough picture taking.

"Okay, not that," Lena agreed, feeling disappointed. She was tired, and hungry, and irritable. She wished the jam were ready, already. It had been sorta dumb to take on such a big project before dinner.

Finally, the jars were boiling.

Abby swung her legs and jumped gracefully off the counter to peer inside the pot that bubbled on the stove. Her face crumpled.

"What? What is it?' Lena looked, too, her eyes widening. The jam had turned a sickening color somewhere between mud and algae. It smelled scorched and bitter.

Abby looked utterly disgusted. "I give up," she said.

Lena was shocked to hear those words come out of Abby's mouth. Any other day she might have been really worried. Today, though, she was relieved. She turned off the giant pot of jars and slipped on a pair of oven mitts. Carrying the jam pot to the sink, she turned on the water and let it liquefy. Watching the gooey mass disappear, she mentally added their failed jam making to the list of things she didn't want to think about.

Lena shut off the water and picked up the phone. "Let's order pizza."

"Makeover time," Abby sing-songed. The pizza place said forty minutes for delivery, so they had time to kill. She steered Lena out of the kitchen so fast, Lena barely had time to put down the phone and grab the camera.

In the upstairs bathroom, Abby lifted her huge makeup bag onto the counter and began pulling out tubes, compacts, pencils, and jars. Abby was con-stantly getting new products that she just had to try out. It was pretty clear that tonight it was Lena who would be the primary guinea pig. She usually resisted, preferring to watch. But right now Lena thought it might be nice to be someone else . . . for a little while. So she sat down on the closed toilet seat and presented her face to her friend.

"I'm focusing on eyes this month," Abby explained as she went to work frosting Lena's lids with a soft mauve. "I'm going to stick with brown tones for you because I think they really bring out your green eyes," she babbled while she dabbed.

"Whatever you say, beauty queen," Lena retorted.

Abby whacked Lena playfully on the arm. "That's Queen Beauty to you," she said, shaking her coiled braids slightly and looking up at the ceiling for dramatic effect.

Lena giggled and turned toward the mirror. She was more than a little curious.

"Oh no you don't," Abby scolded, turning her away. She picked up a liner pencil. "I'm not finished yet."

Lena rolled her eyes. "Can you hurry it up a little?"

"You can't rush an artist!"

Lena sighed and resigned herself to another ten minutes in the hot seat.

Finally, Abby set her last beauty tool down on the counter. "Ready?" she asked.

"Indeed," Lena replied, and stood up to check her face in the mirror.

"Oh my gosh." Lena stared at her reflection. She didn't look ugly. Or totally wacky, as expected. But the dark eyebrow pencil Abby had used on her usually ultralight brows had changed her look entirely. She didn't look like herself. But she looked like someone. . . .

Lena squinted, trying to figure out *what* about her new look was so familiar. She turned her head from side to side, sucking in her cheeks and looking serious — like an angry model.

Abby was staring at her handiwork, too. "You know, you look a little like that guy," Abby said. "The one in your pictures."

Lena stopped goofing and looked closer. Bizarre as it sounded, she actually did. Abby had nailed it. It wasn't exactly that she looked like him though. It was more like he was looking out of *her*. The longer she looked, the more she thought she saw someone else staring out of her eyes.

"You're right," Lena said with a shudder. Her voice was practically a whisper.

Downstairs the doorbell rang, startling them both. Lena let out a whoop and Abby jumped, knocking the box of tissues to the floor, which startled them both again.

"I'll get the pizza," Abby said, recovering first and shoving the tissues into Abby's hand. "You get that stuff off."

Lena didn't argue. She doused a tissue with makeup remover and began to scrub. Several minutes later her brows were their strawberry-blondish selves. Dropping the tissue into the trash, she hurried down the stairs and tried to focus on pepperoni pizza.

Despite the comforting sound of Abby snoring softly, some bad TV viewing, and a bellyful of pizza, Lena could not get to sleep. Every time she closed her eyes she saw the boy in the pictures, or worse, her own reflection with his miserable eyes. Was he becoming part of her? Would she be haunted forever?

Lena shuddered and sat up in the dark. The more she tried to ignore what was going on with the camera, the creepier things got. She may as well try to face it head on. . . .

Lena pulled a flashlight out of her bedside table and grabbed the day's photos off the top. Being careful not to shine the light in Abby's direction, she laid them out on her bedspread. She wasn't sure what she was looking for, but was desperate to find *something*.

Unfortunately, there were no clear signs spelling out cries for help in today's shots, and things that didn't exist were not popping up. She looked carefully at each picture, but not even spooky shadow boy was visible.

"All right, we need to talk," she whispered. "If you want help, you need to stop creeping me out and making weird stuff happen all the time. Got it?" She closed her eyes and tried to relax a little. She must be totally freaking out — she was up in the middle of the night talking to a ghost!

The lack of sleep must have been making her extra nutty. Sighing, Lena moved the beam of light slowly across the row of photos one more time. She paused on a shot of Abby leaning on a tiny, old convertible car. There, in the side-view mirror, was the reflected face of the boy. He *was* there after all! And looking as scowly as ever.

"There you are," Lena whispered. "So what do you want from me? What are you trying to make me see?"

The boy's face was tiny in the small mirror, and

yet remarkably clear — the most in focus he had ever been. Looking closer, Lena could see that he was staring intently at something. She followed his frozen gaze, her own eyes traveling down to the license plate on the outer edge of the shot. *A license plate?* What could be special about a license plate? It wasn't even the entire plate — just a single number: 9.

"Numbers?" she whispered. "You want me to look at numbers?"

Lena's flashlight skimmed over the photos yet again. There were numbers in almost every shot. Quickly, holding the light in her teeth, Lena rearranged the photos in the order they were taken — something she should have done in the first place. "Okay."

Taking them one by one, she wrote down each number she came across on a small pad. The library pic had the number 3 above the door. The shot Abby took in front of the yogurt hut showed three quarters of the address, or 131. The license plate shot included the number 9. And the five-and-dime advertised several 98-cent specials.

Jotting each one down, she came up with 3.1.3.1.9.9.8.

Seven digits. Could it be a phone number? She didn't know of any 313 exchanges in her area, but was considering dialing it to see what happened when the last four numbers — 1998 — jumped out at her. Hadn't the librarian said that the tower was torn down in the late 90s? Wouldn't 1998 qualify?

A shiver ran up Lena's spine. She was suddenly certain that something important had happened on March 13, 1998.

CHAPTER NINE

"Can we just talk about something else for five minutes?" Abby asked through a mouthful of Life cereal. "Like school, or Victor Duenas, or how I am going to convince Mr. Bettendorf to let me codirect the fall theatrical production?"

The girls were sitting at the kitchen table eating breakfast. Lena had barely slept after she'd made her discovery, and it had taken every ounce of her will not to wake Abby up at three thirty in the morning to tell her. But she had resisted, deciding instead to wait until breakfast.

Lena sighed. Clearly, Abby was tired of the Impulse and her theories about being haunted. But Lena's heart had been racing since she'd opened her eyes. She felt wired, ready for action.

In fact, she was surprised she had any appetite at all. She slurped the last bit of milk from her bowl with a nod. "I know this is driving you crazy, but I need to figure it out." She pointed to the row of pictures lying in front of them on the table. "See these numbers? I think they make a date: March 13, 1998. I can't be sure, of course. But I think we should check it out. I mean, it's not like a billion other clues are falling into our laps."

Abby sighed and looked Lena in the face. "This is really eating you, isn't it?" she asked.

Lena nodded, even though she knew the answer was obvious.

"All right," Abby agreed. She chewed thoughtfully and swallowed. "All right, I'm in. Let's blow this pop stand and head over to research central. But here's the deal: We have got to crack this thing today. Or let it go."

Lena laughed a little nervously.

"I'm serious," Abby said. "That camera and this creepy kid are bumming me out. If we can't figure this out TODAY, we are gonna ditch that thing." She thumped the camera, which was (of course) nestled on Lena's lap.

"Bu —"

"No buts," Abby said firmly. "It's outta here. I'll find you another Impulse myself. I'll pay for it. Heck, I'll even go on eBay."

Lena sucked in her breath. Abby really *was* serious. Breaking their strict "no eBay" rule was for genuine emergencies.

Lena swallowed and nodded, but put her hand protectively on top of the camera. One day. They had to sort it out in one day.

You've done impossible things before, she reminded herself, looking around the kitchen. *Like getting this place cleaned up last night.* Between the floor and the stove and the counters and the glop that was supposed to be jam, it had been no easy feat.

The girls loaded their dishes into the dishwasher, waved to Lena's lingering-over-the-newspaper mom, and made their way out the door (escaping before her dad appeared and noticed that half of his last flat of peaches had disappeared). It was a little cooler today, thanks to a few clouds and a breeze that kept the air from becoming too stifling.

Strapping on their helmets, the girls hopped on their bikes and zoomed down the driveway onto the

elm-lined street. Seven minutes later they were locking their bikes to the bike rack in front of the gray stone building.

"There's nobody here," Abby said, looking around. Usually, they had to squeeze their bikes onto the library's jam-packed rack, but today it was empty.

Lena whacked her forehead with the palm of her hand, feeling like an idiot. It was Labor Day, a federal holiday. The library, like the banks and the post office and every other government facility, was closed. "Dang it!" she shouted in frustration. School started tomorrow. She only had one day to put a stop to this haunting business. Besides Abby's twenty-four-hour time limit, being haunted and having to deal with homework would be completely impossible.

"What do we do now?" She turned to Abby, only to discover that she wasn't next to the bike rack anymore. "Abby?" she called.

"Over here," Abby replied. She was at the library door with her face pressed to the glass. "I think someone's in there."

Lena hurried over and followed suit, smashing her nose against the glass. Sure enough, there was a light on inside, and someone was behind the information desk.

"Can you tell who it is?" Lena asked, squinting. Only a couple of lights were on, and it was hard to see.

"Oh my gosh!" Abby cried, jumping back from the window. "It's him!"

Lena's blood ran cold. "The boy?"

Abby barked out a laugh. "No, no," she admitted. "Not *him*, him. It's the cranky library guy."

Lena let out her breath and let in her disappointment. So much for that. "Oh," she said.

"I don't care who it is," Abby declared. "We need to get to that microfilm. It's do-or-die." Not waiting for her friend to reply, she pounded on the door.

"This oughta be good," Lena mumbled under her breath. She knew from past experience that Weird Beard was lacking both a razor and a sense of humor.

The man behind the desk glanced toward the door, then got back to whatever it was he was doing.

Abby pounded again. The librarian looked up a second time and frowned. But he set aside the book he was holding and started toward the door.

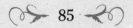

"Let me do the talking," Abby said, squaring her shoulders and looking formidable.

"Sure thing," Lena replied nervously. She was not anxious to be grumped at by Captain Whiskers.

It took the man what seemed like forever to unlock the door. "We're closed," he blurted. "See the sign?" He pointed to the neatly printed sign: CLOSED IN OBSERVANCE OF LABOR DAY.

"I know," Abby said. "And we're so sorry to bother you. But we have an important research project to complete, and were here yesterday but didn't get enough time with the microfilm. Is there any way we could come inside for just a little while? We don't need to check anything out."

"We're closed," the man repeated flatly. His graying whiskers stuck out at all angles.

Lena adjusted the duffel on her shoulder and, feeling disheartened, stared at the stain on the man's shirt. She'd seen similar splotches on her dad's jamming aprons — a fruit stain, probably strawberry.

Hmm.

Before she could think twice, Lena reached into Abby's bag and pulled out a jar of peach jam that Mr. Giff had given her. "Could you open for us, for just a little while, in exchange for a jar of homemade peach jam?" she asked, holding it out and smiling widely.

Abby looked offended. *That's my jam!* her eyes shouted.

I'll get you another one, Lena tried to tell her telepathically.

The man eyed the jar, his expression changing. "Peach, eh? My mother used to make peach." He took the jar and held it up to the sunlight. The yellowy-orange preserves practically shimmered in the daylight. "Only question is, what kind of peach?" He raised an eyebrow like it was a trick question.

"Fay Elberta," Lena replied without missing a beat. "Picked on Friday, and jammed on Sunday."

The man closed his hand around the jar and smiled. His sky-blue eyes twinkled. "I figure this jar of jam is worth about an hour of Labor Day microfilm time. After that I'm going home to have toast and jam for lunch." He winked and held the door open wide.

Abby gave Lena a "you're a miracle worker" look as she slid inside the building.

"Thank you!" Lena said gratefully as they made a beeline to the little room and the microfilm file cabinet.

"Nice job," Abby said as she pulled the first half of 1998 out of the drawer and carried it to the machine. "But you *definitely* owe me a jar of jam."

"Don't worry, I know where there's a fresh supply," Lena replied with a laugh.

"How'd you know that would get him, anyway?"

"The strawberry stain on his shirt," Lena boasted. "My dad has a zillion of those." The sweet success made her a little giddy and she checked herself, remembering why they were there in the first place.

Abby slid the film into one of the machines and switched it on. "What's that date again?"

"March thirteenth," Lena said quickly.

The film zoomed forward at a dizzying rate. Abby released the lever a bit so she could check the headers. February 21. She sped it forward. March 2. Forward again. Lena could feel her heart pounding. March 18. Back. March 14. Back again. March 13.

GARBAGE STRIKE AVERTED read the headline. Lena scanned the front page. There was an article about a business merger, and another about city plans for a new bike path in Narrowsburg. Nothing about a young boy.

Lena exhaled her disappointment. She'd been so sure. . . .

"Hey, wait," Abby said. "If the thirteenth is the date that something important happened, it wouldn't be reported until . . ."

"The next day." Lena's pulse quickened as Abby slowly moved the film forward.

And there it was, in huge, bold letters. Just looking at it made shivers run up Lena's spine. ACCIDENTAL DEATH A TRUE TRAGEDY. The face in the photo next to the headline was unmistakably the boy who had been showing up in their pictures — the only difference was that he was smiling.

"Robert Henson," Abby read the name of the ghost who was haunting them.

Robert Henson, Lena repeated the name in her mind. It felt good to put a name to a face.

According to the paper, Robert Henson fell to his death on the evening of March 13, 1998, from the Phelps water tower. "Police cite unusually slippery conditions on the metal structure due to the icy rain that had fallen that day," the article read. It went on to say that Robert was an only child, who lived with his mother in Phelps. "A quiet boy who kept to himself, Robert did well in school and loved photography." Lena's skin prickled as she skimmed the rest of the article. "We are very proud of our

Robbie," his grandmother stated. "We will miss him very much."

"The poor kid," Abby breathed. "And look at this." She pointed to the next article on the screen.

PHELPS WATER TOWER: TREASURED LANDMARK OR UNNECESSARY HAZARD?

Apparently, the people of Phelps had been arguing about the removal of the water tower long before the boy fell off of it. Some felt it was an important historical landmark of the area. Others maintained it was a safety hazard — an unsafe place where teenagers inevitably gathered. It was likely, the article said, that Robert Henson's death would lead to the tower's demolition.

Everything was connected! The end of Robert was the end of the tower. Still nothing was explained — it was just all tied up.

Lena looked back at the first headline, her eyes resting on the picture. The dark eyes were unmistakable, even without the scowl. And though Lena was glad to see that the boy wasn't always miserable, seeing his smiling face made her realize just how miserable his ghost was.

"Robbie Henson," Lena said, aloud this time.

"I feel like I've heard that name before," Abby said. "Like, recently."

Lena drummed her fingers on the desktop. "Robbie Henson . . . Robbie Henson." She closed her eyes and pictured the name spelled out in her head. For some reason the words appeared typed, but not like they were in the newspaper article. It was kind of an artsy font. . . .

Lena opened her eyes. "The photo contest!" she exclaimed. "He's the guy who won the contest two years in a row!"

She jumped to her feet and pulled on Abby's arm. "Come on — we've got to get to the gallery."

CHAPTER TEN

Abby printed out the two articles, and the girls hurried out of the microfilm room.

"Thank you so much," Lena said as they passed the information desk.

The librarian checked his watch. "You ladies work fast," he replied, setting his stack of books aside. He escorted them to the front door, and after a couple of clicks and turns, released them back into the September morning.

"Enjoy your jam," Abby said with a wave as Lena began to unlock the bikes.

"I most definitely will." He chuckled to himself and closed the door.

"I think you've broken the ice with Captain

Whiskers," Abby said as she grabbed the handlebars of her bike and wheeled it off the rack.

"Come on, slowpoke!" Lena called from up ahead. She was out of breath from pumping so hard, but her body seemed to be on autopilot. They had to get to the gallery!

"What did you put in your cereal, girl?" Abby panted as they raced up Main Street.

"Milk!" Lena replied over her shoulder with a nervous laugh.

The girls skidded to a halt in front of the Barloga Gallery and parked their bikes. Before Abby could even get the lock out of her bag, Lena was pulling open the door.

"You go ahead — I'll lock up," Abby offered sarcastically to her friend's disappearing back.

Inside it was quiet, so quiet that Lena was sure anyone in the gallery could have heard her thudding heart. But the place was empty — even the gallery owner was nowhere in sight.

Abby caught up, out of breath, and the two hurried to the wall of photos at the back of the room.

"Robbie Henson," Lena confirmed, reading the

little plaque below the photographs. She was right —
it was the same boy!

"Interesting kid," a voice said from behind.

Both girls jumped.

Abby found her voice first. "You knew him?" she
asked, looking up at the tall, salt-and-pepper–haired
man they'd seen the day before.

"I did indeed. In fact, I'd say I knew *both* of them."

"Both?" There were *two*?

"Don't look so startled," Mr. Barloga said to Lena
with a gentle smile. "I can explain. You see, as the
owner of this gallery, I always judge the contest
myself. I do it blind, which means that I never look
at the names of the photographers while choosing
the winner, for fear it might influence my decision.
I certainly never intended to pick the same photographer two years in a row. When Robbie came into
the gallery after winning the second year, I was
shocked — for two reasons. The first was that I had
chosen the same boy twice. The second was that he
didn't even *seem* like the same boy. In one year he'd
changed dramatically."

"He's dramatic, all right," Lena said darkly.

"Changed, like how?" Abby wanted to know.

"Here, I'll show you." Mr. Barloga pulled out an

album filled with newspaper clippings and photographs, all seeming to have to do with the yearly photo contest. In the 1996 clipping, Robbie was standing with his parents next to his prize-winning photo, the one with the three pairs of feet dangling off a dock. His smile was so wide, Lena had to look at his eyes to make sure he was the same boy. The picture from the 1997 clipping was starkly different. Robbie stood with only his mother beside the prize photo — the one of the coffee-stained napkin. A deep scowl marked his face. Lena knew that scowl well, and looking at it now made her feel as though she were standing in a walk-in refrigerator — chilled to the bone.

"See what I mean? He looks like a different person. I had no idea I was awarding the prize to the same boy. Never would have guessed. Still wouldn't, I don't think."

"I don't think I would have either," Abby agreed.

"He was a talented kid. Absolutely loved to take pictures, from what I understand. Though I've also heard that wasn't all he liked to take."

Lena's head snapped up. "What do you mean?"

"Well . . ." Mr. Barloga paused, seeming to choose his words carefully. "There were rumors in town.

Things tended to go missing when Robbie was around. Small things, mostly. Trinkets. He got chased out of a few shops in Narrowsburg, and didn't seem to have a lot of friends. . . ." He trailed off, and a worried look came across his face. "But . . ."

But what? Lena stared at the picture in the scrapbook trying to see . . . something. When she finally did, it was as obvious as the nose on her face (or the camera around her neck). Robbie was wearing the Impulse! *Her* Impulse. Or rather, she gulped looking down at the gray box, *she* was wearing *his*.

Abby saw it, too. She shot Lena a sideways glance.

"Anyway, it doesn't matter now. The kid had a great eye. No doubting that," Mr. Barloga went on. "It was such a shame, his dying so young."

Lena stared at the Robbie in the second picture. Except for his menacing expression, he looked pretty much like a typical preteen in jeans and a T-shirt. He wore a crooked baseball cap on his head and carried a yellow duffel over his shoulder.

Lena blinked. The duffel! The yellow duffel! She'd seen it before, and she knew where it was.

All she had to do was go and get it.

CHAPTER ELEVEN

The N16 bus to Phelps was not exactly crowded. Besides the driver, a woman holding a paper sack of groceries, and a guy texting with such ferocity you'd think he was sending Morse code, Lena and Abby were it. They had been unbelievably lucky with the timing, too. It turned out the N16 traveled from Narrowsburg to Phelps three times a day, and they had been able to catch the second bus just outside the gallery with only a ten-minute wait.

"Do you think I should ask to borrow his phone so we can call my house?" Lena asked, pointing at the texter.

Abby wrinkled her brows, which meant, *probably*. But what she said was, "We'll be fine. Everyone thinks we're hanging out in town — and we are. Only it's a different town. We'll be back before they even realize we were gone."

Abby was right. They *were* fine. Phelps was familiar territory, and only twelve miles from Narrowsburg. Nothing was going to happen, and they'd be back by dinner. Still, Lena felt a little guilty. She didn't usually take off without telling her parents. But the truth was, she couldn't risk having them tell her she couldn't go. Time was running out. She had to get her hands on that yellow duffel! And getting on a bus to Phelps was the only way to make that happen.

Even before Abby laid down the law and put the one-day limit on the mystery, Lena had been anxious to get to the bottom of this. Since she'd woken up she'd been overwhelmed by a new urgency. She felt like Robbie was with her all the time now, and not just in the pictures. It was as though she were walking with a strong wind at her back. She felt pushed, and whether or not she *wanted* to move forward was irrelevant.

The girls lapsed into silence as the bus rolled along the road between the two towns, stopping here and there to pick up and let off passengers. The lady with the groceries got off in the middle of nowhere. Two teenagers swung aboard, their chatter mixing with the hum of the bus engine. The guy with the phone lost his signal, leaned his head back, and was now snoring softly. Lena stared out the window, trying not to think about going back to see the shop owner. She definitely wasn't looking forward to *that*.

The pines and oaks and maples began to give way to farming fields, and Lena felt her pulse quicken. They were getting close.

"Is that it?" Abby asked. "Is that the field where the tower was?" Pressing her face against the window, she let the cool of the glass sink in to her skin and stared. All of the strawberry fields looked pretty much the same. But the one the bus had just stopped beside was eerily familiar. There were the roses, and at the end of the field, the shuttered U-Pick shack. It could definitely be the field, and there was only one way to find out.

"Take a picture," Abby prodded.

She didn't need to make the suggestion — Lena already had the camera raised. She peered through the viewfinder and pushed the button. After waiting impatiently for a moment, she pulled the film from the Impulse with trembling fingers while the bus rumbled on.

Lena didn't take her eyes off the developing shot.

"Well?" Abby leaned in and the two of them hunched over the image, staring hard as colors began to appear. Oh so slowly the tower Lena had captured nearly a week ago began to take shape.

"Now you see it," Abby whispered.

Lena looked back over her shoulder to make sure she wasn't out of her mind. No tower. She would have been able to see it rising above the fields even as they pulled farther away. All she saw was September haze. "Now you don't," she said softly.

"Lena, look." Abby tugged Lena's sleeve, bringing her attention back to the photo. "*He's* there, too."

Sure enough, Robbie had shown up in the picture as well. He was tiny, standing on a small walkway that circled the metal bulb at the top of the tower. He was really far away, but it was clearly Robbie. In fact, Robbie was the most in-focus part of the image. He was staring — not out at them like he usually did, but at something in his hand. The look on his face could only be described as intense.

Lena gulped, struck by a revelation. "That's where I fell from," she gasped. "I was up there."

Abby sat back and gave Lena a "huh?" look. "Uh, I hate to point out the obvious, but how could you have been 'up there' when the tower was torn down years ago?"

"In my dream." Lena explained quickly. She wanted to get that information to her friend before her eyes popped out of her head or she asked the bus driver to take a detour to the psych ward. "That's where I climbed in my dream." Lena nodded, thinking back. Robbie must have wanted her to see something in the tower. Only, how could she when the tower was gone?

"This is us." Abby reached up and tugged the cord that lit the STOP REQUESTED sign at the front of the bus. They rolled to a stop at a crossroad. The doors opened, the girls clambered off, and the bus huffed a hydraulic sigh before leaving them in a cloud of dust and fumes. The air cleared to reveal Ruth's Thrift, the shabby-looking shop they had visited several days before. It looked as though it had been waiting for them.

Lena braced herself and without a word the girls crossed the street and made their way up the cracked walkway. When the door opened, Lena exhaled. She had not realized that she'd been holding her breath. In the back of her mind she'd been worried that the store would be closed, or perhaps not really there at all. Or maybe those were hopes instead of worries.

The bell hanging over their heads rang loudly and the old woman behind the desk lifted her head. Her brow was furrowed. She didn't look at all happy to see them.

"Back again," she muttered.

Abby raised an eyebrow at the lackluster greeting and mumbled something about the feeling being mutual. Normally, Lena would have laughed or elbowed her best friend, but something had caught her off guard. She stood there and stared at the old woman behind the desk. There was something in the way she looked at them — something familiar — that had Lena frozen in her tracks.

With a light shove, Abby got Lena to take a few stumbling steps forward. "Where are we headed?" she prompted as they made their way through the musty store. Her patience seemed to be wearing thin.

"Over here," Lena whispered as she led Abby to

the shelf where she had found the camera and remembered seeing the bag. It was still there — the yellow duffel — nestled beside the stack of tattered *National Geographic* magazines. "It's right here." She started to reach for it when a voice behind her made her jump.

"That bag is not for sale!"

The shop owner had followed them. Her voice was scratchy with disuse and startled Lena so badly, she knocked several magazines off the shelf and nearly dropped the duffel.

Without another word the woman snatched the duffel from Lena's hands.

CHAPTER TWELVE

The gray-haired woman loomed much taller than Lena expected. She was faster than Lena expected, too. Lena had flinched when the woman's hand shot out to pull the bag away from her.

But Lena's reflexes were quick, too. Without thinking, she'd reached out and grabbed ahold of one of the duffel bag handles. She had to have that bag!

For a long moment the two stood, each grasping one handle, staring hard at each other. It was a standoff.

"Uh, Lena . . . ?" Abby said cautiously, backing away. "I think maybe it's time to go. . . ."

Lena had other ideas. She held the old woman's gaze, noting the dark intensity of her eyes, and felt the same weird déjà vu she'd had when they'd walked in. There was something here. A connection, or . . . She shivered, unable to put her finger on it.

Whatever it was, it ran deep.

"I need it," Lena said, pulling the bag closer. As she said it she knew it was true. She *needed* the bag, or something inside of it. The angry intensity of the woman's stare made Lena's voice quaver. "It's for Robbie," she ventured uncertainly.

With those words the old woman's eyes changed, just as they had the day Lena bought the camera. It was like watching a cloud pass over the sun. The searing anger turned to gray sadness, and she dropped the handle, staggering back as if Lena had pushed her.

That was a risk, telling her the truth about why we're here, Lena thought as she gently grasped the old woman by the elbow, steadying her. "He needs our help," she explained.

"Robbie." The woman breathed out the boy's name and closed her eyes. She brought her hands together, holding her left ring finger, and gave a slow nod. "Robbie," she sighed again. "He's gone, you know."

"We know," Lena replied gently.

Still the woman kept her eyes tight shut. She looked like a little kid making a wish. Lena and Abby exchanged worried glances, but a moment later the woman straightened and her eyes fluttered.

"I know. He needed help," she said at last, gazing into Lena's eyes. "I just wish I could have been there for him when he was alive."

"So you knew him?" Abby blurted.

"Of course I knew him," the woman replied. "I am Ruth Henson. Robbie was my grandson."

All at once Lena understood why she had gotten that déjà vu feeling. Robbie had his grandmother's dark, intense eyes.

"I believe we could all use a little explanation," Ruth said. "Why don't you girls come with me?"

Abby's eyebrows shot up so high, they practically touched the colorful necktie encircling her hair. But she was silent as she followed Lena and the woman through a door at the back of the shop marked DO NOT ENTER.

"Have a seat." Mrs. Henson directed the girls as they stepped into a kind of parlor. Lena glanced around and spotted a small kitchen off the room they were in and a hallway at the other end. This was obviously where Robbie's grandmother lived — the rooms of the house that weren't part of the shop.

Abby crouched on the edge of a faded couch. Her eyes darted around the room nervously.

"I'll get us a little something. Then we can talk," Mrs. Henson said. She shuffled in her house shoes to the kitchen and began to rummage around.

Sinking down beside Abby, Lena felt her friend's body tense. Abby was ready to make a break for it. And, Lena realized, now might be their only chance. Mrs. Henson was busy and in another room, and Lena was still holding the yellow duffel.

A back door at the other end of the parlor looked as though it opened onto a small yard on the side street. It probably wouldn't be difficult to get away, and Lena could tell from Abby's caged-animal expression that she desperately wanted to escape.

But Abby had promised to devote one day — today — to this haunting craziness. And they were so close. Lena had to stay, had to do everything she could to get to the bottom of this mess. For herself. And for Robbie.

"I'm sorry if I startled you when I grabbed the bag," Mrs. Henson called from the kitchen. "I've been a little rattled ever since I sold you that camera.

Even after all these years it's hard to let Robbie's things go. I've already lost so much. . . ." Her voice trailed off, punctuated by the clatter of dishes.

Lena and Abby were silent. The bag on Lena's lap was still zipped, and it took all of her restraint not to open it and peek inside — the clue they needed could be inches away. But it wasn't hers. Not yet.

"He had it with him when he fell," Mrs. Henson said matter-of-factly. Lena felt goose bumps rise on her arm as the woman appeared in the doorway with a tray of glasses and some juice. "The police gave the bag and the camera to his mother, but she couldn't keep them, so she left them here."

Mrs. Henson set the juice on the table and sat down across from them in a sagging wingback chair that had once been a bright royal blue. "I didn't even realize that old camera was out there." She gestured to the door that led to the shop out front. "Since I live and work in the same house, things seem to spill over from one side to the other."

The girls could have guessed as much. The living room, though small, looked a lot like the store — filled with knickknacks, porcelain figures, and spice tins old enough to be antiques — the kind of stuff that could be treasure or junk depending on your point of view.

A few dusty photos sat on a bookshelf, reminding Lena of why they had come back to Phelps. And it suddenly occurred to her that the bag was not the only place to look for clues. Essential information might be locked in Mrs. Henson's memory.

"Mrs. Henson? Can I show you something?" Lena asked timidly. She reached into her messenger bag and pulled out the Polaroid pictures.

Ignoring Lena's question, Mrs. Henson brought up what had clearly been on her own mind since the mention of her grandson. "How do you know about Robbie, anyway?" she asked, squinting at the girls. "He was about your age when he . . . passed away, but that was probably before you were even born. He would be twenty-five this November the fourth."

"Well, we saw his pictures," Abby explained, being intentionally vague.

Lena cut to the chase. She held out the photos she had taken, the ones with Robbie in them. "These," she said. She laid them out in order, noticing again how Robbie's image became clearer — more in focus — with each shot.

Mrs. Henson put on her reading glasses and took a close look at the images.

"But Robbie . . ." She looked at the girls, clearly bewildered. "He can't be . . ." Her eyes welled with tears.

"We know," Lena replied gently. "It's sort of crazy, but he keeps showing up in my pictures. I think . . . I think he might be haunting us."

Mrs. Henson stared at Lena for a long time, her dark eyes boring right into her. Lena shivered slightly but held the woman's gaze. A single tear slid down Ruth's wrinkled cheek.

"He was a good soul," she finally whispered. "Just misunderstood. And terribly shy. I think that's why he liked his camera so much — it put a little distance between him and the world. He was always happiest when he was behind it."

"He doesn't really seem —" Abby interrupted, but Lena nudged her to keep quiet. Mrs. Henson was on a roll, and it would be best to just let her keep talking.

"After his father left, he stopped smiling. He stopped trusting people, I think. And that made it even harder for him to make friends. He even told me once that he didn't need friends — just his camera." She shook her head. "Of course that wasn't enough."

Lena pretended to drink her juice. Abby did the same, and Mrs. Henson got up and walked over to a tall, painted bookshelf against the wall. She ran a wrinkled finger along a row of brown vinyl photo albums, clearly looking for a particular one.

Above the shelf was a small window with a deep sill. The sun streamed through the glass, catching the light of tiny, colored bottles arranged across it. The bottles stood side by side, pressed close together, with an odd gap here and there where a bottle might have fallen or been removed.

Mrs. Henson sat down and began to flip through the album. Abby craned her neck for a peek, but Lena's eyes kept darting back to the collection of bottles on the windowsill.

"This isn't the one." Mrs. Henson got up to retrieve another album, slipping the first one back onto the shelf.

Though she tried to resist, Lena found herself raising the camera toward the light and snapping a shot of the bottles. Abby looked at her strangely as the camera spat out a square of film. Mrs. Henson, still over by the bookshelf, didn't seem to notice.

"Here it is," the woman called. She turned with a second album open to a page of family photos — Robbie in better days. There were all the typical things you would see in a family album: Robbie in diapers, Robbie and his mom at the zoo, Robbie studying a starfish with his father, and several birthdays sprinkled throughout.

Mrs. Henson touched the photo of Robbie and his dad. "His mother never understood him, really," she said thoughtfully. "She's so outgoing — loves to be with people. Robbie was much more like his father, my son the wanderer," Mrs. Henson sighed. "Always with his head in the clouds. That's his problem — he's a dreamer, a dreamer with restless feet."

Mrs. Henson turned another page and Robbie grew older. He was pictured mostly alone now, and sometimes with his mom. The familiar scowl showed in each shot.

"Marie did the best she could on her own," Mrs. Henson murmured. "But after Robbie died, she fell apart. She tried to rebuild her life here, but in the end she packed up and moved away. She felt terribly guilty, of course. And I don't know if any mother recovers from the death of a child. But it wasn't her fault, of course — it was a terrible accident." Mrs. Henson's eyes welled up again.

Lena tried to look away, but found she couldn't. She was staring at Mrs. Henson as she nervously twiddled the knuckle on her left hand. Lena felt nervous, too — twitchy and squirmy like she had invisible wires pulling at her, compelling her to . . . Once again she was not sure what the feelings wanted her to do.

"So when did he start taking things?" Abby asked bluntly, interrupting the silence. "Was it after —"

"What do you mean 'when did he start'?" Mrs. Henson cut Abby off sharply. "Nobody ever proved anything!" She slammed the book shut and gave the girls a withering look. "If you're here to bring up old charges . . ." Her voice was clipped and started to break. She stopped, took a breath, and started over. "Robbie wasn't a thief, and if that's why you've come, you can leave right now." Nobody moved, though Abby looked like she wanted to.

At last the old woman let out a breath that was half sigh and half sob and collapsed back in her chair. The anger that had quickly flared burned out just as fast, and Mrs. Henson buried her face in her hands, shaking her head. "I never believed it. I never wanted to," she mumbled to herself.

"Mrs. Henson, I'm so sorry, I didn't mean to upset you," Abby apologized. She looked helplessly at Lena, her face full of regret. "Maybe we should just forget the whole thing."

Lena gulped. Her mouth was dry. The strings were pulling, and she was losing control. *No*, she thought desperately. *Now is not the time to take a picture!* But the camera was already against her eye. She aimed. She pressed the button. She captured the old woman in anguish.

Mrs. Henson's head snapped up with the flash and whir. Her weary eyes blazed fury. "I think you'd better go," she snarled.

CHAPTER THIRTEEN

"Holy moley, Lena! Talk about awkward!" Abby clutched Lena's hand and pulled her down the cracked walkway, glancing over her shoulder to make sure Mrs. Henson wasn't coming after them. Though it appeared they had gotten away safely, Abby didn't slow down until the thrift store was well out of sight.

Abby laughed nervously as they rounded a corner and stopped to breathe with their backs pressed against the red wall of a vacant brick building.

Lena couldn't laugh. She could barely speak. "I don't know why I did it," she stuttered. "I couldn't stop it. It felt like I was possessed. . . ."

The Impulse still hung around her neck with the picture she took sticking out of it like a tongue, mocking her. She pulled it free. The image was even more haunting and depressing than she imagined — a close-up of a sad, defeated old woman hiding from the past behind wizened hands. Her crooked fingers spread across her face and into her gray hair like a thick web. It was a beautiful and depressing shot. Looking at it made Lena feel caught in a tangle — just like the jeweled butterfly on the ring on Mrs. Henson's hand.

"Hey, paparazzi. Now you're a thief, too?" Abby pointed at the yellow duffel hanging from Lena's shoulder. "I don't think you paid for that."

Lena shrugged off the shoulder strap and stared. "I . . . I didn't. I just took it. I couldn't leave without it. . . ."

"Holy moley," Abby said again. "I don't think you're being haunted. I think you're possessed!" She looked up and down the essentially deserted street before pulling Lena through the door of the abandoned building.

Hiding in the dusty darkness, Lena felt like a fugitive. "We can give it back," she whispered.

"Great." Abby grabbed the strap and started out, obviously ready to get this business over with. "But I'm not knock —"

Lena pulled her friend back by the other strap. "No. I mean after we have a look inside."

Abby's big brown eyes got even bigger in a silent plea. "But that's breaking and entering. Or snooping. Or something. Something bad," she said. "That bag is stolen property."

Lena knew Abby was right. But now that she had the bag, she had no choice but to look inside. It was the reason they'd come to Phelps in the first place. "If we give it back, it's only borrowed," she rationalized. Abby didn't look convinced, but didn't say anything else.

The two dropped to their knees beside the duffel. Lena tugged at the closure. The zipper echoed like a freight train in the silent building, and Lena nervously reached inside and began to feel around.

One by one she laid the bag's contents on the concrete floor and tried to ward off a wave of disappointment. There wasn't much: an Impulse instruction manual, a school ID, a tattered sketchbook, and a battered tin decorated to look like a treasure chest. Her heart thudding, Lena opened the tin. It was empty.

She swallowed, trying to push down her feeling of defeat.

"Now can we go?" Abby asked impatiently, popping up to stick her head out the door. "All this illegal activity is kind of freaking me out."

"Yeah, we can go," Lena said. She shoved the items back into the bag, pausing with the sketchbook in her hand. She hadn't opened it yet. Flipping it to the first page, she thumbed through. "Maybe we should hang on to this," she said so quietly that Abby didn't hear. She didn't know if she could justify keeping it if her friend protested.

The "illegal activity," as Abby called it, was freaky, but it didn't hold a candle to being haunted. Lena pushed the notebook into her own bag. Zipping the duffel shut, she got to her feet and followed Abby into the daylight.

A few minutes later the girls were closing in on Ruth's Thrift, their pace slowing in unison.

"I say we drop it on the porch and run," Abby suggested. "No sense in upsetting Mrs. Henson any more than we already have."

"But what if somebody else takes off with it?" Lena was the one who took the bag; it was her responsibility to make sure it got back . . . with *most* of its contents. "I'll do it," she offered.

"Okay, okay. I'll go with you," Abby agreed, making it sound like Lena was twisting her arm.

They walked the rest of the way in silence. Lena's mind was spinning. They knew more about Robbie than ever, but still had no idea why he was haunting her. What did he need help with?

"Look! It's closed." Abby practically crowed as they turned up the path. A crooked sign hung in the window. "We're in luck!"

While Abby rejoiced, Lena felt her chest tighten. Closed. Apparently, she'd upset Mrs. Henson more than she thought — so much that the woman had closed up shop for the day.

Abby hung back on the path, waiting for Lena to drop the bag on the doorstep so they could go.

"I'll just knock," Lena said. "In case." She raised her fist and struck the door once.

It immediately opened with a jerk. Lena's heart jumped into her throat when she saw Mrs. Henson. Her eyes were red and the look on her face was terrifying.

"I'm sorry, I . . ." Lena held out the bag, unsure of what to say.

Mrs. Henson grabbed it and clutched it close.

Her eyes were locked on Lena's face, but Lena couldn't stop staring at the woman's hands.

"Your ring. What happened to your ring?" she asked. The butterfly ring she had seen in the picture was not on Mrs. Henson's hand. But as soon as the question had been asked, Lena realized that she'd never actually seen it on Mrs. Henson's finger. It had never been there at all — it was only in the picture!

Touching the spot above her knuckle where the jeweled butterfly ring had perched in the photo, Mrs. Henson looked startled . . . and angry. "I've heard enough of your accusations," she spat. "Robbie never would have taken that. Never. His father gave it to me when — oh, why can't you leave him alone? Just let it go!"

She slammed the door hard, forcing Lena to take a step back off the small stoop. The woman's final, angry words echoed in Lena's head. *Just let it go!*

Lena swallowed hard, her eyes welling with tears. If only she could!

CHAPTER FOURTEEN

Shuffling toward the bus back to Narrowsburg, Lena realized that she actually felt worse than she had that morning — a feat she hadn't thought possible. In the last six hours she had taken off without telling her parents where she was going, upset an old woman — twice — and stolen a duffel bag and a sketchbook. And she wasn't any closer to figuring out what Robbie needed or, more importantly, how to get him to stop haunting her!

Lena dragged her feet in the dust beside the road, kicking up brown clouds to match her mood. Abby was uncharacteristically quiet beside her. Everything about her demeanor screamed that she was over the search, the hunt, the haunt . . . all of it.

"Last bus comes in ten minutes," Abby announced, consulting the bus schedule mounted on a signpost at the corner. She turned to lean on the post and pointed across the intersection. "Hey, look."

On the other side of the street, a shaggy-looking teenager was selling late-season raspberries out of the back of his truck. It was the same one they'd seen in Narrowsburg two days before, the one with bottle caps glued mosaic-style all over its metal body. The one that Robbie had "appeared" in.

Lena and Abby crossed the street to get a closer look. While Abby fished around in her pockets for berry money, Lena felt herself leaning in to study the truck.

"These are the last of the season," the berry seller called to them.

"How much?" Abby asked.

Lena barely heard them. The pickup was a marvel, with every inch covered. Now that she was seeing it up close, Lena noticed that it was plastered with more than just bottle caps. There were bits of tile, mirror, and colored glass as well as tiny plastic animals affixed here and there.

"Where do you get all this stuff?" Abby asked as Lena rounded the front.

"On the ground," the guy replied with a grin. "Every bit. It's a rule — anything I stick on has to be picked up. It's my way of recycling."

Abby laughed. "I get it. It's your 'pick up' truck."

Lena didn't crack a smile. She was too busy looking into the truck's cab. The seat had been recovered with some salvage scrap, and the dash was decorated with a myriad of tiny things. The stuff on the inside was more whole than the stuff on the outside. There was a plastic gecko missing a leg, PEZ dispensers, tiny race cars, and more. What held Lena's eye were the colored glass bottles glued in a line over the glove compartment.

"Where'd you get all of those?" Lena asked, finding her voice.

The scruffy teen poked his head around to see what she was talking about. "Those? The bottles? I found them picking strawberries, right around here. There were a bunch of them, and some glass, too. Way out in the middle of Tower Field, I think."

Tower Field! Lena wanted to ask more, but right then the bus roared into view and Abby pulled her away. If they missed the bus they would have more than a little explaining to do. . . .

"Try one," Abby coaxed, waving the basket of water-bottle-rinsed raspberries under Lena's nose. They had made the bus and were safely seated in the back. "Come on. They're soooo good. And I got him to give me two baskets for three dollars!"

"Not hungry," Lena mumbled. She was too wrapped up in her mixed-up thoughts to think about food. She was also a little dizzy, and the lurching bus was not helping. There were so many questions and so many clues, and still so few answers. She felt like a guinea pig on a treadmill, running around and around and getting nowhere.

Without thinking, Lena pulled out Robbie's sketchbook and began to flip through.

"Holy moley. You swiped the sketchbook?" Abby whispered, gathering up a few more raspberries in her red-stained fingers.

"Um. Yeah. I think Robbie wanted me to," Lena replied defensively. It sounded nuts, even to her. "I think it might help us," she said.

Abby sighed and kept munching while Lena

thumbed through the pages, hoping something would jump out at her. Anything. Nothing did. It was mostly a bunch of scrawled notes — ideas Robbie had jotted down for his pictures, and lots of drawings.

After a few minutes Abby stopped eating and got strangely quiet. Lena tried to tune out her friend's irritation and focus on the book. She was running out of time. And Abby would forgive her as soon as she unpuzzled this puzzle, wouldn't she?

The book smelled faintly musty and the pages were stiff but filled with notes and drawings. From what Lena could tell, though, Robbie was a great photographer *and* a pretty decent artist. He mostly drew fantasy stuff — dragons and castles — not really Lena's thing. But even so, the scenes were detailed and evocative and she found herself turning the pages eagerly to see what else she could find. Further in, the pages were covered with tiny still lifes — images of trinkets, like the colored bottles, miniature vases, and figurines — little things.

Near the back of the book, Lena found a couple of postcards. "Look." She handed them to Abby. "From his dad." Abby took them with a heavy sigh.

The truck-stop postcards were signed, "Love, Dad," and that was all. There were no messages, no information about where he might be headed.

Abby licked a lingering bit of berry off her fingers and leaned in to take a closer look at the book, interested in spite of herself. "Wow. He was pretty good at drawing," she noted.

Lena nodded. "And check this out." She flipped back to a page where she had been keeping her thumb. There was a charcoal sketch there that she kept returning to — a picture of a knight on a rearing horse in front of a stone tower decorated with triangular designs, angled like the legs of the water tower. A dragon was emerging from the other side of the page, breathing fire. It was an exciting scene if you were into that kind of thing. But what kept Lena looking was the tower window. Where you might expect to see a damsel in distress, there was only a small chest — a larger version of the tin box they'd seen inside the duffel. The drawing was signed at the bottom, and titled: SAFE IN THE TOWER.

Reading the slanted scrawl, and remembering her awful dream, Lena felt anything but safe.

CHAPTER FIFTEEN

Lena rolled over. Robbie's fantasy drawing flashed in her head, mixing together with whirling images — the actual tower, his grandmother with her head in her hands, the row of little bottles on the scruffy guy's dashboard, and the photos in the scrapbook. She felt like she had dumped a 1,000-piece puzzle out on a table. The number of pieces was overwhelming. She knew they went together, but at the moment it was just a jumble.

The pictures of Robbie in younger, happier days were troubling Lena the most. Robbie certainly looked like a pretty cheerful kid when he was little. It made Lena wonder how it would feel to have one of your parents up and leave. Of course it would feel awful. Horrible. And for a loner like Robbie, probably worse than that.

Just go to sleep, Lena told herself as she rolled onto her other side and closed her eyes. *Time's up. You start school tomorrow!*

On any normal night before the first day of school, Lena would be lying awake thinking about what she was going to wear and who she was going to see. Not this year.

This year, Lena's mind was a tangled mess, and none of the strands had anything to do with first-day jitters. A hopeless feeling came over her in the darkness. Helping Robbie seemed impossible. So far she'd only succeeded in getting more questions, and if Abby stuck to her word, which she usually did, Lena couldn't count on her to help anymore. She was on her own. And *that* was assuming she could keep Abby from taking away the Impulse.

When the morning sun finally spilled its light onto Lena's bed, she threw off the covers and got to her feet. Her head throbbed dully and her body was tired and achy — she felt like she had the flu. She stepped around the library printouts and photos she had spread on the floor before going to bed and pulled some clothes off a chair next to the closet. As she glanced in the mirror, she noted that she didn't look any better than she felt. Her wide-set green eyes had dark circles under them and even her freckles seemed pale.

"Too bad it's not Halloween," she said grimly. "I could go as a raccoon." Maybe she should call Abby and request a quick makeover before school. . . . She could really use her best friend right now.

Right on cue Lena's door burst open, revealing none other than Abby herself. "Ready for our first day of sev — yikes, Lena," she blurted, interrupting herself. "You look like you've been up all night!"

Lena tried to smile but grimaced instead. "I'm all right," she said feebly.

"No, you're not. But if I have anything to say about it, you will be. Pronto." Springing into action, Abby whirled around the room, retrieving everything that had anything to do with Robbie Henson — the photos, the sketchbook, and the library printouts.

Panic rose inside Lena, squeezing her lungs and making it hard to breathe. *Time's up,* she repeated to herself.

When Abby had gathered everything Robbie-related, she stuffed it unceremoniously into her bag and gave Lena a long, hard look. "I am hereby forbidding you to even think about anything that has anything to do with this spooky Robbie business," she announced. "You hear that, Rob?" she called to the ceiling. "I am exorcising you!" Then she cracked a smile. "You don't want to flunk out of seventh grade over the ghost of some dead kid, do you?"

"Definitely not," Lena replied honestly. But she was also pretty certain that it wasn't up to her! Abby was a force to be reckoned with, but Robbie was a *ghost* — a ghost capable of haunting someone and making her do all kinds of crazy things, like steal sketchbooks!

Abby planted one hand on her hip and extended the other one expectantly.

"What?" Lena asked, widening her eyes innocently. If she pretended to have forgotten the details of the deal they made, she might be off the hook.

"Um, the Impulse?" she said, as if it should be obvious. "The one you promised you'd hand over?"

Lena held her hands over the Impulse protectively. Funny . . . she hadn't even remembered putting it on. "This old thing?" Her voice cracked.

"Here." Abby retrieved Lena's digital from her

desk and offered it in trade. "You can still take pic-tures, just not, you know, *his* pictures."

"But, I . . ." Lena racked her brain for something to say . . . a reasonable argument for keeping the camera. Only there wasn't any, because nothing about being haunted was reasonable.

Feeling a simultaneous flash of resentment and frustration, she forced her hands to lift the strap over her head. She must have looked tortured, because before she got it all the way off, Abby gave in. A little.

"Oh, forget it," she said, putting the digital back on the dresser. "I guess I can't deprive you of your art. But no more talk about towers or helping ghosts. And no taking the camera to school. Deal?"

Lena gulped. "Deal," she said quietly as she set the camera on her dresser. She felt odd and shaky without it, and for five full seconds neither girl said anything.

Then, with a quick glance at Lena's clock, Abby was back in action. "Wowza. We'd better get moving. Horace Brighton Middle waits for no one."

Lena pulled on her backpack and started to fol-low Abby out of the room. Then, at the last second, something made her turn and grab the camera off her dresser.

"Thanks, Robbie," she whispered. At least they agreed about one thing — the Impulse belonged with her. She stuffed it deep in her pack and promised herself she wouldn't take pictures.

In the kitchen Abby forced a banana into Lena's hands. "Eat this," she said, grimacing at Lena's exhausted face. "Maybe a little potassium will help." She opened the fridge and poked around, finally emerging with a bagel and a package of cream cheese. "No time for toasting." She sliced the soft bagel in half and spread it with a generous amount of cream cheese. "Breakfast of champions," she said, handing it over.

Lena raised an eyebrow.

"Okay, maybe not. But it will get you through your first homeroom of the year, and if you're lucky, all the way to lunch."

Lena forced a laugh and took the bagel. "Thanks, *Mom*."

"You're welcome, *dear*," Abby replied, leading her friend out the door.

The air was still cool and the girls decided to walk fast, so that Lena could have time to eat. They waved to a group of girls up ahead and did their best to avoid being run down by Josh Windham and his skater crew as they flew past on their boards.

When they finally stepped onto the school yard the place was in a state of first-day chaos, which meant that things weren't as crazy as usual. The sixth graders were totally new, and looked sort of confused and worried. The seventh and eighth graders were clustered in small groups, talking and laughing with quiet excitement. Even Josh and the other skaters were holding their boards instead of riding them.

"Two weeks from now this scene will be totally different," Lena noted as the first bell rang.

"Indeed," Abby confirmed in her best Principal Cohen voice. The two girls started up the stairs with the orderly throng of middle schoolers. "None of these children will be following the yard rules, pandemonium will ensue, and detention will be given appropriately."

Lena giggled and slipped inside the door, passing a pack of sixth graders who had no idea where to go.

Thank goodness this isn't my first day at Horace Brighton, she thought gratefully, remembering how nervous she had been when she'd started middle school. *That, on top of being haunted, would definitely put me over the edge.*

"Hurry up," Abby said, waving a piece of paper in the air. It was the letter the school had sent the week before with her class schedule and locker assignment. "I need to find locker 218!"

Since locker assignment was alphabetical at HB Middle, Lena and Abby would never have lockers right next to each other. Still, they were dying to know where they'd end up.

"I'm 242," Lena said. They made their way down the hall with the rest of the students, hunting for their lockers.

"I'm over here!" Abby called, stepping to the side of the hall.

Lena tracked the numbers on the other side. 238, 239, 240, 241 . . .

"We're right across from each other!" Lena half shouted through the throng. Total score!

After pulling out her locker assignment sheet, Lena twirled her combination dial, and was struck by the happy realization that since she'd left her house she'd felt fairly normal. She looked around the hallway and smiled. Maybe school was the answer to her haunting problems. Maybe Robbie would disappear right along with summer. The guy couldn't fault her for paying attention to her teachers, could he? Reaching into her pack, Lena toyed with the idea of leaving the Impulse in her locker. She started to pull it out, then decided not to mess with a good thing. She felt okay, didn't she?

"You ready, or what?" Abby leaned next to Lena and eyed the swarms of passing kids. "What's the holdup? You can't be finishing your homework," she joked.

Laughing nervously, Lena pulled her hand from her bag. Her thumb tangled in the Impulse's strap and it flopped out, too. Her secret was revealed!

Biting her lip, Lena waited for Abby to say something.

The bell rang. They had to get to class. Abby was silent.

"See you at lunch?" Lena mumbled.

"Yeah, see you." Abby disappeared into a cluster of kids. Lena slammed her locker closed and made a beeline for class, trying to ignore the cold feeling in the pit of her stomach. She wasn't sure which was worse — being haunted or getting caught lying to her best friend.

All things considered, Lena did a decent job keeping her mind on her schoolwork. It helped quite a bit that Miss Jones seemed to be the best English teacher ever, and that they were starting to read *Chasing Redbird* by Sharon Creech, one of her favorite authors. And that Mr. Greene, her science teacher, had some interesting plans for learning about cells.

But by the time she got to lunch, all Lena could think about was the look on Abby's face when she'd seen the camera strap. Scanning the crowded room for her friend, she stepped into the lunch line. She was digging around for change in the bottom of her bag when her fingers brushed across the smooth, familiar surface of one of her Polaroid photographs. Before she could stop herself, she'd pulled the photo out of the bag.

Glancing down at the image, she was instantly irritated to see that it was the shot she took of the window of Don's Pawn. And there was Robbie, reflected in the corner of the window, looking intense as usual. Lena felt anger rise in her stomach at the sight of him. Hadn't Abby given him the brush-off? Why couldn't he go haunt someone else? The sun glinted off the glass storefront in the picture, making most of the dusty junk on display almost impossible to see while highlighting a gaudy row of jewelry. What was that weird-looking thing in the center, anyway? Some kind of insect?

Lena was about to chuck the photo into the nearest trash can when everything kind of shifted and her blood ran cold. No, it wasn't an insect. It was a butterfly. A butterfly ring. The same butterfly ring that had shown up on Mrs. Henson's hand in the photo she took at the old woman's house — the one with the giant opal in the middle.

Jerking her head up, Lena scanned the lunchroom for Abby a second time before she realized that even if Abby were standing right next to her she couldn't talk to her about the ring. All things Robbie were off-limits.

There was only one thing to do, and she would have to do it alone. Lena left her tray on a nearby table and darted out of the lunchroom.

CHAPTER SIXTEEN

The buzzer sounded as Lena entered the pawnshop and she shuddered as she stepped inside. It wasn't hard to remember why she didn't like the place. It smelled like cats and mildew and hard times, and before the door even closed behind her the shop-keeper was giving her an unfriendly once-over.

"What do you want?" the skinny lady croaked from a stool in the corner.

Lena shoved her hands in her jeans pockets and stepped sideways, craning her neck to see the tray of rings in the dusty window. Sure enough, the butterfly ring was there, resting between a pewter-and-pearl number and the biggest (and ugli-est) fake diamond ring Lena had ever seen. The butterfly's body was a long opal, and even under a layer of dust Lena could see the pearly stone's strange patterns and multicolored hues. She had always loved the way opals seemed to glow — like they had rainbows trapped inside. The wings of the insect were rimmed with gold and littered with colorful, inlaid gems.

Nine out of ten people would have called the ring tacky, but Lena could not take her eyes off it. It had a beauty all its own and it made her feel happy and sad at the same time. Happy because the ring was actually here. It existed, and she knew it was special. And sad because even though she wasn't sure how or why this ring was so important, Mrs. Henson had obviously been missing it for a long time.

"How much is that one?" Lena asked, pointing to the butterfly ring.

The woman grunted and reluctantly came out from her perch behind the counter. She looked Lena up and down a second time and seemed to come to the conclusion that the girl didn't have enough money to buy it. With a bored expression she reached into the window, pulled out the ring, and examined the tiny tag.

"One hundred and fifty," she announced. She eyed the ring scornfully for a moment before putting it back — without giving Lena a chance to take a closer look.

Lena felt a flash of irritation. She wanted to hold the ring, if only for a few seconds. But she didn't protest. What was the use? A hundred and fifty dollars was more than she had. A lot more. "Thanks," she said a little sarcastically. Lena could hear her mother in her head telling her not to be rude, but she couldn't help it. She was disappointed, frustrated, and exhausted. Besides, the store clerk wasn't exactly friendly.

Lena turned to go.

"I told my husband we'd never sell that thing," the woman said to Lena's retreating back. "I told him that when he bought it."

Lena pulled her hand off the door handle. She hadn't even thought to ask where it came from, or how long it had been here!

"Do you remember who he bought it from?" she asked, suddenly feeling a little breathless. "Was it a boy, around my age . . . only a long time ago?" She couldn't imagine Robbie selling his grandmother's ring, but knew that desperate people did desperate things. Maybe he needed some cash really, really badly.

"It was a while ago, all right," the woman confirmed. "Only it wasn't *a* boy. It was a *bunch* of boys. And they were older than you. They had a heap of funny things to sell, right around the time we bought the place. Late nineties, I guess. I thought the stuff might be stolen, but they claimed they found it in some demolition site over in Phelps. Sounded fishy, but it's not my job to investigate the history of every little item that comes through here. Everything but the ring sold that first year. That insect has been sitting in the window collecting dust for a decade. Probably be here until we retire, because nobody's ever gonna buy it."

The woman had turned around and was talking to herself now as much as to Lena. "That's why I do the buying now," she groused. "That's how it should have been from the beginning. . . ." She settled onto her stool in the corner and an orange-and-white cat jumped onto her lap. The woman waited for the feline to settle and began to stroke her back.

Lena reached for the door handle, pulled, and stepped into fresh air. Whew, that was better. She checked her watch. There were twelve more minutes of lunch — she'd have to hurry to get back in time.

Half running, half walking up the sidewalk, Lena

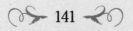

let her mind work along with her legs, in fits and starts, lurching along, connecting the dots. Selling a ring to a pawnshop with "a group of boys" sure didn't seem like Robbie's style. Nevertheless, he could have been involved.

As she rounded the corner, Lena's train of thought jumped the tracks as she almost ran right into Abby. "Whoa," she called out in spite of herself, her cheeks reddening. She had broken her promise not to think about anything related to Robbie, and now she'd been caught — for the second time that day. She had to turn the tables, fast.

"Hey. Where've you been?" Lena asked. She tried to act casual, like she always spent her lunch period downtown.

A guilty look flashed across Abby's face, then disappeared. "Nowhere," she replied with a shrug. "Where were you?"

Lena wanted to tell her friend the truth, but didn't dare. "Nowhere," she answered instead. It was true, in a way. Because that was exactly where she was getting with this whole Robbie thing.

Nowhere. And fast.

CHAPTER SEVENTEEN

"Give it back. Give it back." The words echoed in Lena's head while she slept. In her dream, Mrs. Henson was yelling at her from the castle window. At least, she thought it was Mrs. Henson. Was it Mrs. Henson? Yes — Mrs. Henson in Abby's Boy Scout cap. Weird.

"I didn't mean to take it," Lena shouted in reply. But the wind carried her words in the opposite direction — she was too far away. Suddenly, a figure charged toward her from the base of the castle — Robbie riding a shrunken bottle-cap truck as if it were a horse. He carried the Impulse, aiming it at her like a weapon. His lips moved frantically.

Lena resisted the urge to run. She needed to hear what Robbie was saying. He charged closer and closer, and Lena braced herself, willing her legs not to move. Then, finally, she could hear him. "Help me," he said. His eyes were desperate, pleading. "Give it back."

"We have to give everything back," she announced, barging into Abby's room. She felt pretty awkward, because she and Abby had barely spoken all week. But her latest nightmare had set her on a new path, and she needed Abby's help.

Abby was still in bed. She barely moved under the covers. Lena glanced at the clock. It was 7:32, ridiculously early for the first Saturday of the school year, and even more ridiculously early to be waking up your currently estranged best friend.

"Um, I mean, sorry to wake you up so early. But I need all the Robbie stuff so I can send it away."

Abby threw back the covers and sat up. "Finally!" she crowed, looking up at the ceiling. "The girl has come to her senses!"

Lena sheepishly dropped the cardboard box she was carrying and looked around the room. It was a disaster area — piles and piles of stuff. Magazines, clothes, books, dishes, and more clothes — many of which Lena recognized from their thrifting adventures. Her dresser was covered with every kind of concealer, powder, blush, eye shadow, eyeliner, lip liner, and mascara ever created. The floor was practically invisible. Lena clucked her tongue. "Girl, how do you find anything in here?"

Abby yawned and got to her feet. "I don't, usually," she admitted. "But you already know that."

Lena used a foot to gingerly lift a heap of clothes, then threw up her hands. "Well, I need you to find that sketchbook. I'm sending it back . . . along with my Impulse."

"Really?" Abby raised an eyebrow.

"It's the only way I'm going to actually sleep again in this lifetime."

"Right. But what about Ghost Boy?"

"I think this is what Robbie wants."

"Excellent!" Abby beamed. Then her face fell. "But what about all that free film?"

"I don't know. Maybe I'll give it away," Lena replied. "I can decide that later. Right now I need to know where the stuff is. . . ." She looked around the room worriedly. "Do you know where you put it?"

"Of course I do," Abby replied, sounding a little offended. She got to her feet and picked her way across her room to the closet. Shoving a pile of books aside, she opened the door, turned on the light, and disappeared inside. A moment later she reappeared with a pile of stuff.

"Here you go," she said, handing it over.

"You can toss the photos," Lena said, taking the sketchbook and dropping it into the box as if it burned her fingers. Then, before she could change her mind, she set the Impulse on top, shoved in a bunch of crumpled-up newspaper, and closed it up. "Packing tape?" she asked.

Abby unearthed a pair of jeans from a pile next to her bed and slipped them on. "Downstairs," she said, pulling her sleep tee over her head and donning a turquoise blouse instead. The bright fabric looked great against her dark skin. Checking her braids in the mirror, she nodded approvingly and added gloss before stepping over several mounds on her way to the door.

Abby found a roll of packing tape in the laundry room junk drawer and a mailing label in the family room desk. "Let's see if we can look up the address," she said, switching on the now-functioning computer. She typed in "Ruth's Thrift" and "Phelps, NJ" and hit ENTER. A moment later the address appeared on the screen.

"We could probably just send it to Ruth Henson in Phelps and it would get there," Lena said as she copied the address onto the label. "But I don't want to take any chances. The last thing I want is to see this box back on my front porch. Or anywhere else, for that matter." She smoothed the clear tape across the top of the brown cardboard. It was ready to go.

Lena felt a pang of sadness but shook it off, remembering the dream. As much as she loved that Impulse, she had to give it back. Wasn't that what Robbie — and Mrs. Henson — had told her to do? "I'm going to drop it off at the post office right now, then head to Saywell's for breakfast. Wanna come?" She felt oddly shy asking. "I'll buy — it's the least I can do." It wasn't quite an apology, but she hoped Abby would understand her intent.

Abby grinned and licked her lips. "Mmmmmm, ricotta pancakes," she said. "You're on."

* * *

That afternoon Lena helped her dad process the final pounds of peaches for jam. With her hands in a bowl of blanched, overripe O'Henrys, she peeled the damp, fuzzy skins away from the luscious insides. Her hands dripped with juice and the sunny smell of ripe peaches wafted past her nose, and still the cold spot inside her could not be warmed.

Lena heaved an inward sigh. She'd thought that everything would be all right once she mailed the camera and the sketchbook, but without that camera around her neck she felt a little . . . naked. Not to mention sad. Of course it was great to have her friend back, but the rest was so unresolved. And her mind kept drifting back to Robbie. Would he ever get the help he needed?

"I'm short!" Lena's dad suddenly cried. He smacked his hand on the counter, making Lena jump.

Lena glanced up from her pile of peaches and eyed her father's six-foot-four frame. "Actually, Dad, you're pretty tall," she retorted.

Lena's dad chuckled. "No, no. I mean I'm short on fruit — I need more peaches. How about another trip to Phelps? They might have a few stragglers. We could go tomorrow morning. . . ."

Lena felt a cold shiver run through her. She shook her head. "No, thanks. I have, uh, plans tomorrow." That wasn't exactly true. In fact, she had no plans at all for the following day. But she didn't want to go to Phelps. Not tomorrow. Maybe not ever.

Lena peeled the last O'Henry and plopped it into the bowl. The pile of shiny, juicy fruit was impressive.

"Anything else, Dad?" she asked.

Mr. Giff shook his head. "No thanks, honey. I'm just going to pulp these babies up and put them in the fridge for tomorrow."

Rinsing her hands in the sink, Lena felt anything but peachy. Slowly, she climbed the stairs to her room. Plopping onto her bed, she gazed out the window at the cloudless sky. It was a gorgeous day, sunny and crisp, and yet she felt as gloomy and heavy as lead. She had done exactly what Robbie and Mrs. Henson had asked her to do in the dream. So why didn't she feel even a little bit better?

Rolling away from the window and onto her back, Lena spied the one picture Abby hadn't confiscated sitting on her bedside table — the window at Don's Pawn. Lena picked it up and looked at it for what felt like the hundredth time. The ring was still there, and as she studied the picture she began to see something she'd missed before. . . .

Robbie was in the picture, which she already knew. But now she noticed that his hand was carefully cupped as if he were holding something, but his palm was empty. His gaze, intense as ever but also full of longing, was resting squarely on the butterfly ring in the window.

Help me, his voice said, clear as anything, in Lena's head. *Give it back.*

CHAPTER EIGHTEEN

"So what's the big surprise?" Lena asked, sliding onto a stool next to Abby at Saywell's Soda Fountain the following Saturday.

Abby looked like she was about to burst but remained silent as she pointed to the swinging door.

"Someone's coming?" Lena guessed.

Abby shook her head.

"There's something outside?" Lena tried again, attempting to squelch her frustration. She wasn't much of a guesser.

Abby shook her head.

"I give," Lena said. She could tell her best friend was seriously excited, and she wanted to be excited, too. But she still wasn't sleeping much. She'd tried her best to convince herself that she had washed her hands of Robbie, that she had done everything she could to help him. But the image of the ring and the boy's desperate refrain were still troubling her.

You don't have a hundred and fifty dollars! she told herself. And stealing the ring was out of the question — her thieving days were over, not to mention the high security at Don's Pawn. She had to let it go.

"The contest! The contest!" Abby finally erupted with the news she'd been dying to share. She pointed to the flyer on the door. "You won the contest!"

Lena stared at her friend in shock, her mouth hanging open. "That's impossible. I didn't even enter."

"Oh yes, you did," Abby corrected. "I entered one of your photos on the first day of school, and it was chosen. You won!"

Lena was still for a moment, trying to let this information sink in. The prize money for the contest was two hundred dollars — serious cash. It was more money than Lena had ever had at once. More money than she had ever spent.

More than enough to do what she needed to do.

*   *   *

Even though she was expecting it, the sound of the buzzer made Lena jump. She staggered into the dimly lit pawnshop, out of breath from biking all the way home to bargain with her dad, then turning around and biking all the way back to town. But she was also elated, because after seeing the contest winner announcement Abby gave her, her dad had agreed to loan her the prize money in advance, which meant she had exactly two hundred dollars in her pocket.

"I'd like to buy that ring in the window," she said.

The woman looked up, surprised. "You're going to spend a hundred and fifty bucks on that bug ring?" she asked with a skeptical squint.

Lena's smile stretched from ear to ear. "Well, I didn't say that. . . ."

CHAPTER NINETEEN

"There it is! There it is!" Abby tugged on Lena's arm, dragging her over to where her prizewinning picture was hanging. This wasn't easy since the gallery was crowded with folks eating tiny appetizers and sipping wine and sparkling water from little plastic glasses.

Dazed, Lena allowed herself to be led through the crowded room.

Suddenly, Abby stopped in her tracks. "Act natural," she said, smiling at an elderly couple who were also moving in the direction of the winning photo.

Lena bit her lip and tried to look like an artist — creative, cool, and appropriately aloof. She felt anything but.

"She's the winner!" Abby blurted to the passing couple.

"Congratulations," the white-haired woman said. "I just love that photo. So moving, so real. Tell me, did your subject have to sit for long?"

Lena smiled graciously at the lady. "No, it was just candid, actually. A moment I felt compelled to capture on film."

"Well, it's wonderful," the man agreed as the couple moved away.

"Come on, the coast is relatively clear," Abby said, tugging Lena over to her photo. The poignant moment of Mrs. Henson's anguish was no longer a floppy Polaroid image. It had been blown up and framed, and now hung proudly on the gallery wall.

Lena looked at the photo and smiled despite the sad subject matter. It was, she knew at once, the best photograph she'd ever taken — the photo of a woman hiding behind her wizened hands. She felt proud — proud of the photo, and proud of helping Robbie at last. Finally, that great weight had been lifted.

Still, as she gazed at the photo, Lena couldn't ignore a pang of sadness that stemmed from knowing that the camera she'd captured it with, Robbie's Impulse, was gone forever.

"Don't worry, we'll get another one," Abby said, reading her mind. "I just saw one on eBay last night for forty bucks, and according to my calculations that's just about what you have left over after buying that ring... which, by the way, was totally nuts."

Lena smiled slyly. "Actually, I have a little more than that."

"No." Abby looked dumbfounded. "You haggled? At Don's?" Her smile grew as she spoke. Her eyes sparkled and she beamed at Lena with newfound respect. "How much?"

"One twenty-five," Lena replied proudly.

Abby laughed. "Looks like my reign as haggle queen might be ov — !"

"Hold it right there." A gravelly voice interrupted, freezing Abby and Lena in their tracks. "Now, say cheese."

They turned slowly to see Mrs. Henson, all dressed up and holding the Impulse — Robbie's Impulse — up to her eye. On her finger she wore her butterfly ring. On her face she wore a smile.

Lena grinned back as the old woman pushed the

button. Mrs. Henson had obviously found the gift Lena had left on her front porch the night before, the one she'd carefully wrapped in a flyer for the gallery event.

As soon as the picture had popped out of the Impulse, Mrs. Henson lifted the strap from behind her neck and placed it over Lena's head. "Robbie would want you to have this," she said warmly. As she stepped back, she smiled and twisted her ring around her finger.

"And he would have wanted you to have that," Lena said, gesturing to the butterfly. The pearlescent jewel gleamed in the gallery light, throwing off sparks of color. "I don't think he meant to take it, really. He just wanted to keep it safe, and then . . ."

"Yes, yes, I know," Mrs. Henson said, her eyes glistening with tears. Lena understood. Mrs. Henson was happy to have the ring back, but would give it up in a flash for just another moment with her beloved grandson — a moment to tell him that she forgave him for taking the ring, that she loved him no matter what.

Lena reached out and took Mrs. Henson's hand. "He knows," she said softly. "He knows how much you love him."

"Of course he does," Mrs. Henson agreed with a sniffle. "And I can't thank you enough for helping him. For helping us."

"You're welcome." Lena felt the familiar weight of the Impulse around her neck, and noted that the cold feeling in the pit of her stomach had melted away. She felt warm all over.

Beside her, Abby bounced back and forth on the balls of her feet, looking from the old woman to Lena and back. "So, Robbie's Impulse is yours to keep?" she babbled.

Lena recognized the crazed look in Abby's eyes right away. She had seen it hundreds of times before.

"Does this mean what I think it means?" Abby asked, clearly unable to contain her excitement.

Lena grinned and patted her pocket. "Yes, indeedy," she declared. "Cash in pocket."

"Time to hit the thrift!" Abby hopped up and down.

"I can offer you a twenty percent discount at my store," Mrs. Henson said with a laugh.

"We'll take it!" Abby said. She held out her hand and they shook on the deal.

Lena looked down at the just-developed photo in

her hand. There she stood with Abby, both of them grinning from ear to ear. And in the reflection of the glass of her now prizewinning picture was another, familiar face — Robbie's. But instead of a scowl, her unhappy ghost wore the biggest smile of all.

BITE INTO THE NEXT POISON APPLE,
IF YOU DARE. . . .

"You are going to *die*," my best friend, Tasha, said. Her brown eyes were wide with horror.

I laughed. "You're being ridiculous."

Tasha made a face. "You'll be lost out there. And I won't survive here without you."

We were sitting under a big oak tree on the grounds of our school, eating sandwiches. The sky was blue, the sun was sunny, and warm breezes lifted strands of curly brown hair from my ponytail. It was a perfect September day.

School had been back in session for two weeks, and it seemed like Tasha and I had spent most of that time having the same conversation. Tomorrow, I was leaving Austin for three months, and I couldn't wait.

"You love Austin!" Tasha insisted, tucking her chin-length black hair behind her ear and making a sad face at me. "And seventh grade has already started! We need to be study partners! And plan the Halloween Dance together!" She crumpled up her empty chip bag and looked at me, lips trembling. "Marisol, you *can't* leave. You won't be able to make it out in the middle of nowhere."

Tasha is very, *very* dramatic. One day last year, she called me crying so hard she couldn't talk. I thought she was sick, or that something had happened to her family. I rushed over to her house on my bike, but it turned out she had just gotten a bad haircut. And it wasn't even that awful!

Tasha being her dramatic self made me reluctant to show any nerves at all: If I was the level-headed one, I wasn't going to admit to any doubts about leaving town. And it's true I love

Austin. My hometown is the best city in the world —
you can walk or bike pretty much everywhere; it's
beautiful; and there are terrific restaurants, funky
coffee houses, great hiking trails, and cool music.
And I wasn't leaving forever — I'd be back in just
three months.

But sitting on the lawn looking at my best friend's
sad face, I knew she wasn't going to be able to even
pretend to get excited for me. I also knew that admit-
ting even the smallest case of nerves would totally
set Tasha off on another rant, which would only
make me more anxious. I swallowed the last bite of
my sandwich and reached out to squeeze her arm
confidently. "Tasha, I'll be back before Christmas."

Tasha sighed and looked at me sadly. "I'm going
to miss you."

Of course, I knew that was what she'd really been
saying all along. Still, it was nice to hear it. I hugged
her. "I'll miss you, too, Tash," I said. "But we'll both
be fine. We'll talk and text and e-mail. Just think of it
as if I'm on a really long vacation."

I went to sleep that night with my bags packed, gazing up at the glow-in-the-dark stars on my ceiling

and trying to think of it just that way: like a vacation. But Tasha's words had affected me more than I thought they had. As I lay in bed listening to the footsteps and laughter of passersby outside my building, I felt a cold shiver of anxiety. I'd pretended I was one hundred percent excited about going to Montana in front of Tasha, but I *was* a little nervous. I mean, who wouldn't be? Sure, stepping into the unknown might be an awesome adventure, but it was also *scary*. I drifted off to sleep uneasily, an anxious knot in my stomach.

A minute later, I was outdoors. The air was crisp and clear. I was walking along a wooded mountain path, brushing easily past the branches of wind-twisted trees. Dry leaves crunched under my feet. Above me, the sky darkened, but I wasn't worried about getting lost. I knew, in the way you always know things in dreams, that I was in Montana, exploring, and my heart was beating fast with excitement, not fear.

I reached a clearing in the woods and gazed upwards. Cygnus, Aquila, and Ursa Major — familiar constellations — shone overhead, seeming so near I almost believed I could reach up and touch them. Just above the top of the trees a huge yellow full moon drifted in the sky.

Behind me, leaves rustled. I turned in time to see something disappearing into the undergrowth. Was it a cat?

I took a few steps forward. Yellow eyes gleamed at me from the bushes. A coyote? I crouched to peek beneath the bush. Whatever was in there whined — a thin, lost sound.

The breeze was rising, turning into a wind. On the wind, I heard, faint but clear, Tasha's voice again, much more ominous than her joking tone earlier: "You're going to die."

Suddenly, I was afraid.

I started to run, and, as I ran, I could hear something coming behind me. I didn't want to look back.

The path ended abruptly at the edge of a cliff. I wobbled at the brink, catching a dizzying glimpse of rocks and water far below, before turning and looking back. I had to see what had been chasing me.

There was nothing there. And then I fell.

CANDY APPLE BOOKS
Read them all!

Drama Queen

I've Got a Secret

Confessions of a Bitter
Secret Santa

Super Sweet 13

The Boy Next Door

The Sister Switch

Snowfall Surprise

Rumor Has It

The Sweetheart Deal

The Accidental
Cheerleader

The Babysitting Wars

Star-Crossed

www.scholastic.com/candyapple

How to Be a Girly Girl in
Just Ten Days

Accidentally
Famous

Accidentally
Fooled

Accidentally
Friends

How to Be a Girly Girl in
Just Ten Days

Miss Popularity

Miss Popularity
Goes Camping

Making Waves

Juicy Gossip

Life, Starring Me!

Callie for President

Totally Crushed

Wish You Were Here,
Liza

See You Soon,
Samantha

Miss You, Mina

Winner Takes All

POISON APPLE BOOKS

Miss Fortune

Now You See Me...

THRILLING. BONE-CHILLING.
THESE BOOKS HAVE BITE!